T0025547

William Melvin Kelley

Dunfords Travels Everywheres

William Melvin Kelley was born in New York City in 1937 and attended the Fieldston School and Harvard. The author of four novels and a short story collection, he was a writer in residence at the State University of New York at Geneseo and taught at The New School and Sarah Lawrence College. He was awarded the Anisfield-Wolf Book Award for lifetime achievement and the Dana Reed Prize for creative writing. He died in 2017.

By William Melvin Kelley

A Different Drummer

A Drop of Patience

dem

Dancers on the Shore (short stories)

Dunfords Travels Everywheres

Dunfords Travels Everywheres

WILLIAM MELVIN KELLEY

ANCHOR BOOKS
A Division of Penguin Random House LLC
New York

FIRST ANCHOR BOOKS EDITION, SEPTEMBER 2020

Copyright © 1969, 1970 by The Estate of William Melvin Kelley
Illustrations copyright © 2020 by Aiki Kelley

All rights reserved. Published in the United States by Anchor Books, a division of Penguin Random House LLC, New York, and distributed in Canada by Penguin Random House Canada Limited, Toronto. Originally published in hardcover in the United States by Doubleday, a division of Penguin Random House LLC, New York, in 1970.

Anchor Books and colophon are registered trademarks of Penguin Random House LLC.

This is a work of fiction. Names, characters, places, and incidents either are the product of the author's imagination or are used fictitiously. Any resemblance to actual persons, living or dead, events, or locales is entirely coincidental.

Portions of this book originally appeared in *Playboy* magazine, copyright © 1968 by H.M.H. Publishing Co., Inc., *Negro Digest* and *L'Arc*.

The Library of Congress has cataloged the Doubleday edition as follows:
Name: Kelley, William Melvin, 1937–2017.
Title: Dunfords travels everywheres / William Melvin Kelley.
Description: First edition. | Garden City, N.Y., Doubleday, 1970.
Identifiers: LCCN 70118849
Classification: PZ4.K285 Du PS3561.E392
LC record available at https://lccn.loc.gov/70118849

Anchor Books Trade Paperback ISBN: 978-1-9848-9937-8
eBook ISBN: 978-1-9848-9938-5

Book design by Anna B. Knighton

www.anchorbooks.com

Printed in the United States of America
10 9 8 7 6 5 4 3 2 1

I dedicate dhis Book
t'Jessica Gibson Kelley
n Cira Tikaiji Kelley,
two o'dFamily's many Travelers.

The Futurafrique, flight-furbished ebony astride
velvet-paved miles, vies with the
sunflower magnificence of the
Oriens, challenges the snow-lily
diadem of the Europa. . . . . .

——MELVIN B. TOLSON

The language in which we are speaking
is his before it is mine . . .
I cannot speak or write these words
without unrest of spirit.
His language, so familiar and so foreign,
will always be for me an acquired speech . . .
My soul frets in the shadow of his language.

—JAMES JOYCE

We slept in that bush, but when it was about two o'clock in the night, there we saw a creature, either he was a spirit or other harmful creature, we could not say, he was coming toward us, he was white as if painted with white paint, he was white from foot to the topmost of his body, but he had no head or feet and hands like human-beings and he got one large eye on his topmost. He was long about ¼ of a mile and his diameter was about six feet, he resembled a white pillar. At the same time that I saw him coming toward us, I thought what I could do to stop him, then remembered a charm which was given me by my father before he died.

—AMOS TUTUOLA

Dunfords Travels Everywheres

1

BOY! Chig! Wake up and move over. Please."

Sunday: Chig Dunford, Frank, Lane and Wendy shared the small sedan's backseat; Ira, driving, Marian beside him, and Cleurdia rode in the front. Under hot plastic, Chig felt the steel ribs of the automobile's side against his left hip; he did not answer.

"Hey, Chig, you deaf? Move over." Lane laughed. "Wendy's hips are sharp as needles."

The car's passengers squirmed, knowing the story. Lane had slept with Wendy for three months. Then, at the beginning of the summer, she had broken off their affair, but had taken no one new. She and Lane continued to see each other at little Gallery openings, at the Café of One Hand for Sundays of softball. All agreed that she acted decently toward him. But Lane kept snipping at her, especially about the pointed edges of her body; today, her hips.

"Nothing to move over to, Lane. You'll just have to suffer." Immediately, he regretted using the word, suffer. He did not know if Wendy found him attractive, but hoped she did, and tried always to say things that pleased her. Now, foolishly, he had agreed with Lane about her hips.

"Hold your shirt; we're getting there soon." Ira had never slept with Wendy. He had lived with Marian for two years. Besides, Wendy seemed not to like men who grew mustaches.

"I'll bleed to death before that." Lane went cleanshaven.

"That's not a bad way to die." Chig could not see Wendy's face, only her bare legs, two sets of knees away in the cramped backseat and very long, tanned the color of natural beige leather. For the past few weeks, she had been in Spain, had just returned, looking healthy. This Sunday, she wore yellow shortshorts.

Lane had not answered. Perhaps by commenting openly on their bodies, Chig had gone too far.

He had created a silence, and tried to decide whether or not to speak. Usually, when one of his friends created a silence, Chig would break it. This time, he would have to wait until their feelings subsided and one of them spoke.

He turned away, looked out the open window. They travelled up the Beulward dol Touras, one of a kind of long, broad avenue Chig had found in every European city he had visited. But Chig considered Beulward dol Touras, lined with tall oaks, more majestic than most.

Many cafés fronted the beulward under the oak trees. In each café, by use of a bell-bedecked white wire supported at one end by a ring in the outside wall of the café, and at the other by a white standard, the management had divided the sidewalk tables into two sections.

On the right side of the ringing wire, the native men and women of that country wore suits, jackets, pants, dresses, skirts and shirts in hues and mixtures of blue and red. On the left side, the natives wore combinations of yellow and red. Neither side's colors appeared all bright, or drab, all new or all old; but when Chig squinted, the colors blended that way.

One of that country's oldest traditions, many foreigners found it difficult to understand. None of the natives on either side of the wire owned wardrobes composed entirely of one side's colors. In the morning, each native in the country would pick an outfit for that day. He might choose blue-red or yellow-red, making himself, for the day, an Atzuoreurso or a Jualoreurso.

In the street, each native lived the day his morning choice had dictated. The government reserved parts of the subway and autobus for Atzuoreursos, parts for Jualoreursos. Employers divided their offices and factories in this way. No citizen worked at a permanent desk or machine. Each used that section of the room where The Morning Choice, Lua Madjona Cheursa, had led him. Most married couples wore the same colors, to ride public transportation or take coffee together. Some couples did not, leading separate lives until they had returned home, locked their doors, and disrobed.

Four or five of Chig's twenty or thirty friends had tried to live by the tradition, dividing their closets and making their choice. But soon, each and all found it impossible to continue; some situation always developed which forced them to cross the white wire. Still, they tried their best not to disturb the natives. If, as a body, they attended a movie or a play, they would decide beforehand to dress either Atzuoreurso or Jualoreurso.

Sunday, for softball, they chose Jualoreurso.

Marian turned to look at him, forgave him first. "Are all the windows open, Chig?"

He had rolled down his window at the beginning of the ride; salty exhaust from the cars ahead cooled his face. He nodded.

Marian's unbuttoned pink shirt did not hide her large, soft breasts, little more than the nipples under a small yellow biki-nibra. "You think I'll get a real tan today?"

"It all depends on the sun, Marian." He always felt uncomfortable when his friends talked about skin.

"I wish I had an all-year tan." Her teeth had grown in crookedly. She had told him her braces pained her so much that she tantrumed until her parents ordered the dentist to remove them.

Chig smiled, the only thing to do. "You might not like it, Marian. It's all right to get a tan at the resort. But it ain't so good to arrive there with one already."

They all laughed, especially at his ain't. Serious people, they had all come to Europe for very much the same reason: home troubled them.

"Anyway, you're really a beautiful color, Chig." An artist, Marian used a lot of brown in her work. Several times, he had visited her and Ira at their studio in the Old City.

"I wish more people felt that way."

All of them nodded, except Cleurdia, a native. Sometimes she seemed not to understand them. When a person talked directly to her, she caught almost everything. But when the conversation did not involve her, English held less meaning for her than the barking of dogs.

Marian rested the tip of her chin on the top of the front seat, hiding her breasts for the moment. "But still, things are getting better, aren't they, Chig?"

"Sure. Don't you think so, Chig?" Lane leaned forward, answered for him, then waited for his answer.

They all waited. He wondered what would happen if he did not answer, but dared not risk it. "Well, the President is pushing some strong stuff through Congress."

"That's true," Frank agreed. He sat squeezed between Chig and Lane. "The man is a master-politician."

"But that's not what Chig meant when he said things were getting better." Lane had forgotten that he answered Marian's question. "But what about the human heart, Chig?"

They studied him, all except Cleurdia.

"I think he understands the human heart. And he knows he can't change it overnight. He said recently that the future is built on the framework of the past. He's probably building a legal framework first." He hoped they would begin to talk about the President, much admired by people their age.

Most times, Chig tried to answer their questions, to help them understand the experience of Africans in the United States, the pain of slavery, the shame of segregation, the frustrations of integration, and all the rest of it. But this Sunday he wanted only to play softball and store up sun. Summer had almost ended and soon, a long European winter would darken the city. He wanted to take in as much sun as possible.

"That's probably right, Chig." Lane spoke. "But how do you feel now, today?"

"Today, we just have to throw ourselves open to all human beings." Marian sighed; she had explained this many times before. "We have to spread our arms wide and embrace everything people have to give." She addressed Chig. "And then reflect it in our art."

Lane stared at her for a moment. "Ya, sure, I suppose so." He hesitated, then suddenly turned moderator. "Let's hear what Wendy has to say."

Wendy leaned forward, from behind Frank and Lane, into the window's frame. The wind rippled her yellow silk blouse, whipped strands of long black hair across her cheeks. "You remember, Lane. We've talked about it before. That night you said you didn't mind if the Coloreds had better jobs and schools and houses, but that, remember Lane? you resented race-mixing. And we talked and talked. We were looking at the sun come up over the rooftops, and finally I made you see that one of a man's most important rights is to marry anyone he pleases, no matter what color. Remember that night? When your roommate went to Paris?"

"Ya. Sure." Lane nodded. "The human heart."

2

"BUT HE UNDERSTANDS THAT."

"Who understands what, Marian?" From somewhere below Ira's yellow-red plaid shoulder, Chig heard the smack of his hand on Marian's thigh.

"I mean the President, Ira." She answered him, then all of them: "The President." She nodded.

"What about him?"

"He understands, Lane. About the human heart." She bounced in her seat as she spoke. "He's not like the rest of them. He's not a politician."

"That's not true. He's a master-politician. He really is." Frank sat up straight. Costumed completely in brownish-red, shirt and pants, except for a yellow ascot, he looked almost elegant. "I mean he understands the system. He's not innocent."

"Mother says the same thing." Wendy whispered; smoke rose behind Lane's head.

Frank turned toward her, the back of his head neatly trimmed. "I didn't mean it that way, Wendy. I meant he's not politically innocent. He's spent thirty years in the service of government. He understands how it works. He has a vision of where he wants the future to go. He's not just holding the line." Frank compared governments at that country's Uneveurseto Netswonal, spoke the language well enough to do so. One night, several months before, his stomach filled with red wine, he had confessed to Chig that at twenty-six, he remained a virgin. "And he's a master-politician, which I said before."

Wendy reached across Lane and stroked Frank's hand with her fingers. She wore a pale gold wedding ring on her right hand. "I believe I haven't made myself clear, Frank." She smiled; Chig loved her smile, her dimple. "That was only when he first got to Washington. Later, he settled down. He and his wife often spend the weekend with some of Mother's friends. I really agree with you, Frank. And you'd like him too."

"So you know him real well, huh?"

"I honestly didn't mean to brag, Lane. He's Mother's friend's friend." Inside the loose silk blouse, she took a breath. "I've only spoken to him exactly twice in my life, at some teas my parents and I attended. And he was very pleasant. But perhaps your parents know him better."

"They never met him." Lane's father grew tons of wheat somewhere between Chicago and Cedar City; Chig had never known exactly where. "But they know the Vice President, very well."

"Now he's a politician!" Frank commented, beginning to laugh. "I mean in the spirit that Marian meant."

They did not often laugh at Frank's jokes.

"I still don't know how he even got nominated." Marian stared over the back of the seat, down into Lane's lap.

"Here we go again!" Lane slid forward to the Vice President's defense. "You people always talk about how corrupt midwesterners are. Corruption was invented before there even was a Midwest, right on the old East Coast. So don't tell me your Mr. President of the Younger Generation is a lily either!"

"Nobody said he was a lily, Lane." Ira leaned back, shouted at the roof of the car. "He makes deals. But not half as many—"

"That's not true. He was rich before he was elected to anything." Frank fingered a pimple on his jaw. Like dragon's heads, two pimples seemed to erupt for every one he burst. "He didn't have to make any deals."

"Don't be stupid enough to believe everything they tell you in school, Frank." Lane paused. "Everybody's a little corrupt. Right, Wendy?"

"Of course, Lane. But I don't believe I've heard as much gossip—"

"That's only because he covers his tracks better. He's a smart one."

"That's just the point," Ira and Marian chorused.

Frank picked up the thought. "He's smart and he's not interested in just money or power. He'll change things."

"Just as long as you agree he's no lily, like Chig said."

Most of Chig's mind had been outside of the car, in a café with an iced-tea cooling his hand. "I didn't say anything, Lane."

"Someone did." He pushed Frank back into the seat, turned bright blue eyes Chig's way.

Chig shook his head. "No one said he was a lily, Lane."

"Hey, I know what I heard." He continued to study Chig. "Are you saying—"

"Oh, shit!" Ira interrupted. "I forgot the demonstration."

They had stopped. A half-mile ahead, over the shining roofs of several hundred idling automobiles, stood the thirty-storey Touras Netswonals.* In the park at its base, a crowd of natives,

---

* LUAS TOURAS NETSWONALS: Actually three towers in one, a tower of wood within a tower of stone within a tower of brass. According

Jualoreursos and Atzuoreursos both, had gathered to protest the war raging in Asia.

"I'm sorry about this." Ira turned full around and addressed the four in the backseat. "They can't even start the game. We have all the balls." One side of his mustache drooped lower than the other.

"Can't you get out of it some way, for golly's sake?"

---

to recent archeological evidence, the aboriginal tribes of that part of Europe erected the innermost, wooden tower to commemorate an alliance entered into with Attila, King of the Huns (406?–453 A.D.). Until late in the fifteenth century the only place where the native-born could commit suicide without legal or social interference; in modern times, an average of eighty-nine natives jump from the towers each year.

"Look for yourself, Lane." He beckoned around them to the shining cars. "It's not moving. Can I fly over it?"

"It's all right, Ira." Marian kissed his ear; Ira jumped.

"What o'clock is it, please?" Cleurdia did not turn her head.

Snatching his cuff halfway up his arm, Frank told her: 12:40.

She thanked him, twisted to smile at Lane. "In the jeurnala it has said that the manofestatson will finish at two hours o'clock."

Marian sighed. "Over an hour? We'll bake."

Chig did not mind that too much, but already a wet half-moon had appeared under Lane's arm. Frank's face shone with grease. Only Wendy seemed unaffected. She started a new cigaret, blew smoke out of her window.

"Well . . ." Marian leaned forward, and, elbows wiggling, took off her shirt. Chig put on his sunglasses. He had never seen any breasts quite like them, even in films.

LUOS ESTOTOS EURNIDOS SORLIT D'ASHA: Parading a huge sign, a group of students moved among the stranded cars, heading toward the Towers. Attracted by the spots of bright-yellow in the front seat, one student turned their way, then stopped, then stared.

The first student grabbed the arm of a friend, pointed; then ten, then twenty boys had gathered around the car's hood, four feet away, staring through Ira's windshield. Short like most men in that country, they had to stand on tiptoe to see, a group portrait in the front window, their eyes bright, skin pale, long hair covering their ears, pushing and shoving each other for the best view.

"Now, what do they want? Ira, get them out of the way. The traffic might start again." Lane reached over the front seat, waving the students aside. "Hey, Cloode, tell them to get away."

"Put on your shirt, Marian."

"What's wrong, Ira?"

Chig felt embarrassed for her.

Lane leaned across Wendy, began to yell out of the back window. "Vo! Vo!" He tapped Cleurdia's shoulder. "Hey, come on, tell them to move away. Vo, you bastards!"

"Put on your shirt."

"But Ira, I'm so hot." She seemed not to see the students, a puzzled smile on her lips.

"Marian, will you please cover your God-damn tits?"

Frank covered his giggle.

"Why are you shouting at me, Ira?" She fumbled with her shirt, but could not find the sleeves. "Why did you shout at me?"

The students saw her trying to dress herself. "No! No!" Several of them, in the front rank, bent down, grabbed the fender, began to rock the car. "NO! No! NO! No!"

Lane screamed at them, in English. "Hey, Roomps, if you guys want to get physical, we'll get physical. God-damn Roomp bastards!"

Cleurdia turned, offended.

But Lane did not notice; the line of cars ahead began to roll, and behind them, a horn trumpeted the first eight notes of that nation's Anthem. "Come on, Ira, run over them!"

Ira shifted into first gear. "But I don't want to hurt anybody."

Marian had finally buttoned her shirt. Defeated, the students released the fender and stood back. They smiled, waved farewell, as Ira's car started forward.

Turning to his right to watch the students by the window, Chig found Wendy looking at him with her dark brown eyes.

KNOWING THE ABILITIES of the seven stranded in the demonstration, their friends had not waited to choose sides. Arnold Lockman, a can of beer in his fist, stood in the gutter, saving Ira a parking space. He directed Ira's maneuvers, pounced to open the door. "Want some, Wendy?"

"No thanks, Arnold."

"Where you people been?" Arnold had on a short-sleeved canary yellow shirt.

"A gang of Roomps attacked us."

"No kidding. How many of them?"

"Twenty." Lane stretched. "I almost jumped out of the car."

"Then you didn't really fight."

"Didn't have to." He smiled. "Old Ira boy just about ran them down."

"I thought you had a real fight, bud." He drank from the can. "Want some, Chig?"

He shook his head. "It wasn't as bad as Lane said. They just rocked the car."

"No kidding."

Ira opened the car's hood and pulled out the canvas sack which held the bats, bases, balls and gloves. Chig volunteered to help him. Side by side, they dragged the heavy sack the twenty yards between Ira's car and the four bare circles of yellow dirt that their weekly game had worn into the park grass.

They set out the bases, while their friends greeted one another. Frank and Cleurdia passed them on their way to the public toilet house, a half mile away across center field. Every Sunday Cleurdia went there to change into her playing clothes. And Frank usually contrived to go with her, walking beside her at stiff attention, an even two feet from her. Every few steps he would lean toward her, say something, begin to laugh. She never joined him.

"Hey, Chig, heads up." Ira threw the ball.

"I wish he'd just go on and ask her out." Chig pitched wild. "Sorry. She'd go, I think."

"Lane's got that locked up."

"At least Frank could ask her." He wondered when he would ask out Wendy, now that she seemed free. "Lane doesn't care about Cleurdia."

"Frank'll just keep cracking his bad jokes." Ira smiled. "What a Jew!"

"Frank's not Jewish."

"I know. He's an RC pretending to be Jewish. My father would love him for a son."

"Come on, Ira. You showed me letters from your father." He could not make the ball reach where he aimed it, wished he hit the same way. He always hit high flies to center. "He seems happy with you. You're not a bum. You stay clean. You dress—"

"You don't understand. We're not interested in that kind of thing. That's what they say, but they're the ones who like all that show, parades, medals, image. My father doesn't care how

I dress. I could dress like a bum. If I was a banker. How's your arm?"

"Coming."

"My father takes a real interest in my work. He even knows a little about the art world, who's big, who's small. He used to come by my studio in New York and sit on a stool and tell me I was great. On the way to the States, he had to spend a few years in a couple of European cities. He was on his own and wanted to have a good time and he knew the best-looking girls went with artists, so he went with the artists too. He gave them another name. So he knows what's good, and he says I'm good. Throw the ball."

He did, too high. "So why doesn't he want you to be an artist?"

"I'm wasting my time, he says. Nobody cares about art, Ira. If it was like when I was a boy in Europe and you wanted to be an artist, I'd send you with good wishes. They had some respect for artists there. But Mr. Mustache changed all that. Artist, banker, doctor, bum. Right into the oven. Don't waste your time giving them beauty, he says. Make money. That way, when the pogrom starts, maybe I can buy my way out."

"You're kidding." He laughed again as soon as he had made his comment.

"My father's seen a lot; he's very cynical. I say to him, but Daddy, there won't be a pogrom here. But he answers: We said the same thing in Spain, just before the Inquisition started, to say nothing of Russia and Germany. So I don't argue with him." Ira shrugged. "I know what I'm doing is right. Somebody's got to bring some beauty into the world."

"You fellows working something up?" Lane had jauntied over to them. "We want to start." He stood between them, one hand leather-covered, turning his head from side to side. "You were warming up with the game ball."

"The game ball?" Chig tossed it to him. "Sorry. We didn't mean to hold you up."

"Well, let's start." He escorted them to home plate. There, Chig's friends milled, asking what team each belonged on, and which position, and where in the batting order.

Marian talked with an exchange professor's wife about the students who had bounced the car. ". . . against the States is running high. I think they just got carried away. But there was a strange kind of love in what they did. I mean, they never actually tried—Hi, Chig. And our having Chig in the car showed them we weren't the kind of people they were against." Taking him by surprise, she scooped him close, mashing the bikinibra between them. "Chig's like a good luck wand, charm."

They laughed. The professor's wife, in a yellow-gray denim shirt and pink dungarees, nodded her head.

"We're on the same team, Chig." Ira joined them.

"What about me, Ira?" She released Chig. "Who do I go with?"

He puckered his lips, kissed her. "Could I play against my sweety?"

"Come on, gang, rag or rock them!" Lane led his team onto the field: the male model who played shortstop, the government scholar from Iowa who manned third, a blonde with knobby calves who typed at the Embassy. And Wendy, long straight black hair, tanned legs, yellow shorts over a high round behind, took a position in right field, swept her hair away from her face with two fingers and pounded a pocket into her glove. The others followed. Lane circled around to pat their backs, nudge their elbows. "Rag and sock them!"

Ira started the batting-order, swinging, missing twice before hitting to the male model, who fielded nicely, but threw over the first baseman's head, who retrieved the ball and ran it back to the pitcher. By that time, Ira stood, coughing, on third base.

An architect from Minnesota left him stranded, striking out on three straight pitches.

Chig's turn had come. Before stepping into the box, he looked out at Lane, crouched and playing him deep; behind Lane squatted the public toilet house, the air above it jellied by the sun.

As the first pitch left the pitcher's hand, Frank rounded the building's corner, stumbled, and started toward them, waving his arms.

The pitch bounced on home plate, skittering through the catcher's legs, a ball. Cleurdia too had started across the field, trudging, her head bowed.

"No batter! No batter! No batter!"

Frank ran, flatfooted in a patch of tall grass, his feet tangling. He had already fallen once.

Chig wondered idly if he could hit a ball over Lane's head. Lane never took his eye off the ball; perhaps he and Frank would run into each other. He watched a strike.

Frank had run within thirty yards of Lane, his mouth opening, closing; poor Frank and his jokes.

The next pitch came stomach high and over the plate. Smiling at his own seriousness, Chig swung—watched Lane shuffle forward, stop, looking deep into the sky. Chig started down to first base, watching Frank, ten yards from Lane, a shout in his throat, his hands fisted. "Hey! Time out!"

They collided. For an instant Frank kneeled on Lane's shoulders, a snapshot of a circus act; then they tumbled onto the grass, a heel, an elbow, Frank on his face, Lane on his back.

Chig laughed before anyone else, just because he could not believe what he had imagined actually happened. But within seconds, everybody laughed. Ira stood on home plate, coughing and laughing. Marian had rushed to hug him, but, fighting for breath, he kept pushing her away.

They laughed until Lane crawled over to Frank, pulled him by his ascot, and began to punch at his face. "You made me miss it, you stupid shit!"

"No, wait." Frank tried to defend his face. "I'm sorry, but wait."

Finally Arnold parted them, but not before Frank had started to cry. "The President's shot." Tears, and a little blood from a cut Lane had opened dribbled down his cheeks, dripped to the grass, but Frank smiled. "It's true. He's shot."

Half of Chig's friends laughed again, but not Lane. "You're not funny, Frank. Don't you know that yet, you stupid shit!"

Frank shook his head, his eyes the same as when he had told Chig about his virginity. "But it's true. Last night. Well, about four hours ago."

Chig stepped back from the circle and tried to find Cleurdia. She was in very deep center field, still walking. She had not changed to her playing clothes. He went to meet her. "Shot, Cleurdia?"

She nodded. "He has dead."

"Wow. But how?"

"They have carried guns." She looked at him now, shaking her head. "And also his wife and . . ."

They joined the others. Frank had completed his first report; the blonde with knobby calves sat in the grass, weeping. But most had gathered around Frank and Lane. "Okay, now tell again what the radio said."

Frank sniffled. "Last night, a few hours ago, and that two men came out of each dugout and walked up and shot him. The batboy got in the way . . ."

"How'd they get into the dugouts?"

"They don't know. They were just changing sides and a lot of people were running around because they had some trouble

with the lights, and four men all dressed like groundskeepers and all of them with acorns, I think the radio said, I was
translating, anyway with acorns in their lapels came out of the
dugouts, and walked over to his box and . . . and then they had
shotguns and fired at everybody in the box." His eyes glowed
deep pink like wounds; the little cleft in the middle of his upper
lip had filled with water. "His wife and his two youngest children, and a man who was selling ice cream and a photographer
who was taking pictures of that, with his kids and the ice cream
man, I mean."

"Stick to the point, Frank." Lane punched his glove.

Frank patted himself for a handkerchief, but never found
one. "I am."

"Well?"

"So the President jumped up, I don't know if he was hit yet,
but I guess so with shotguns. He jumped up and tried to get
to the aisle. But then the groundskeepers had pistols, the ones
dressed like groundskeepers, and they shot him." He paused,
hurt already by what he would say. "In the back!"

"Well?"

"And he fell. And everybody was running around, like it
was a riot, the radio said, and the groundskeepers, I mean the
men dressed as . . . they went into the nearest dugout and . . ."

Lane nodded his head. "A professional job, all right."

"Is that all?" Arnold asked.

Frank shook his head. "They caught one."

"Why didn't you say that before?"

"I was coming to it, Lane." He swallowed, cleared his nose.
"They blocked all the exits. And this groundskeeper came out
of the clubhouse and they arrested him."

"What'd he say?"

Frank smiled. "That he was a groundskeeper."

"Is that all?"

"He said he didn't do it. They checked and he is a grounds-keeper, but he's still a prime suspect. Ten years ago, they said, he was one of the leaders of a movement to unionize the grounds-keepers or something like that."

Lane nodded. "That figures."

⟜ 4 ⟞

"WELL, THERE'S NOT very much we can do about it here."
Lane lowered his head for a few seconds. "Chig would've been
out if Frank hadn't barged into me. Who bats now?"

"What do you mean he would've been out?" Arnold asked.

But most of their friends began to pack. Ira held the equipment bag, stuffing it with bases and gloves, then bats and balls.
They loaded into the car, rode within ten minutes.

Ira leaned forward, his chest an inch from the steering post.
"I know it's a little early, but I'd like a drink."

"That's a good idea, Ira." Marian had buttoned her shirt to
the throat. "And let's buy some newspapers."

"Ira? The office of Lua Jeurnala dol Swora," Cleurdia
offered, timidly, "you can found on Beulward dol Touras."

"Come on, Cleurdia, it'll be a mess there. You think it was
bad before?"

"You have a match, Chig?" Wendy sat beside him now.
Lane had jumped into the car first, into Chig's corner, followed
by Frank, then Chig. Wendy had kept her window.

Chig did not carry matches, told her so, smiling. Wendy just looked at him, killed the smile on his lips.

"Here's one, Wendy. The dirty killers!" Frank handed her a striker torn from a matchbook and two matches. "In the back. Who could've wanted to do that?"

"Are you kidding?" Lane laughed. "Don't you read the papers, or just books? We're at war, but you don't know it. Those groundskeepers were probably sent from the other side twenty years ago."

"He wasn't even President twenty years ago."

"Not just to kill him, Marian. To cause trouble when the time was ripe."

"What's so ripe about now?" Chig did not follow politics. The literature of nineteenth-century Europe took up most of his time. "I mean, compared to a year ago."

"Don't you be naive too, Chigboy. You know what's going on in the world."

"Sure, but are we having more trouble with the other side than we've always had?"

"We're having less trouble with them! And he's responsible." Frank's eyes remained red. "They even respect him. They know he's a smart man."

"Was." Lane nodded slowly. "Was a smart man. And if he was so smart, why was it so easy to kill him? Did you ask yourself that, Frank?"

"Even an Einstein or an Abraham couldn't have stopped their guns. Not without knowing the plan, but then they would've failed, right?"

"Ira, I want to be there when you hear the other side did it."

They reached the city; the traffic thickened, little streets packed with little cars, sidewalks shoulder-tight. Many natives that sunny summer Sunday wore their white undershirts, their pants alone telling what choice each had made that morning.

Some already held newspapers at arm's length, squinting at the pages. Others lined up, single file, Jualoreurso, Atzuoreurso, Jualoreurso, Atzuoreurso at news-stands, waiting silently for the latest editions. The city had changed color.

Chig's friends continued to talk as he watched the natives. Then Ira parked, and they climbed out and began to walk the three or four blocks to the Café of One Hand.

They tried to stay together on the hot narrow sidewalk, but groups of natives kept forcing them apart. "Certainly, I have bought already food to last six months." Chig understood them; he had registered at the Esceurla Laungua within a month of his arrival in the city, had done well. "A Commonist? You speak like a silly—something about his face that was not pleasing to me, perhaps—the ears of the regent may thus have found the door of the stable, my sir."

They stopped to buy two native newspapers. Mainly for Lane, Cleurdia read aloud from Lua Jeurnala dol Swora, translating into English: "Winging outside, the performers threw away their gloves of catch into the grass. The President had bend his back into his lap and to writing a small book that have buy it for the occasions, before the contest."

"What?"

"For golly's sake, Frank!"

Frank shook his head. "I'll have to read it myself."

". . . ice of cream two and more times to permit the photographer license to photograph his children."

Marian stopped—Chig bumped into her, his thighs mashing her flat, soft buttocks. She turned to him, showed her crooked teeth.

"Sorry, Marian."

". . . making their walk of death toward him, weapons at the aim. One performer, he a Moorish, questioned by your corospondonto remarked that he had seen a weapon, but he it had believed to be the usual caretaking instrument. It is he telling too the authorities about the acorns the assassinuos weared."

Chig smiled, laughed inside, remembering a poem his father had often recited: Wherever you go, whatever you do, you'll find a Tom, peeping on you.

"To the Giants of Frost, my sirs!" Two Jualoreursos and three Atzuoreursos blocked the sidewalk in front of them. Busy with a wine bottle, they did not see Chig and his friends approaching.

For a moment, the two groups met, merged: "I just bought a Rabbit. Now I am late to break her in." Wendy moved closer to Chig. "To the Giants, then?" Above the drinker's head, the red wine glowed, bubbling inside the shining upturned bottle. "Hear, little pig, is it that you prefer the Eagle to the Wild Boar?"

Cleurdia ignored the question.

"Hear, is it already the Eagle eats the apples?"

Lane stopped, asked Frank what the native had said to him.

"He was asking if we had invaded them."

"What the hell is that supposed to mean?" He glanced back at the natives. A stocky hamster-faced Atzuoreurso stared after them. While they watched, he spat on the sidewalk. "Hey, hold it a second, Ira. Mr. Roomps is looking for trouble."

They stopped. Cleurdia peeked over the paper at each of them, then down the block toward the natives.

"What did they say?" Ira turned around. "Come on, they're booz—"

"They said," Frank explained, "something about our invading them."

"Today we lost our President." Lane addressed Chig. "And I'm in no mood for stupid comments."

Chig studied the natives, who now stood abreast, soldiers in a film about some ancient kingdom. The bottle moved from hand to hand, waist high, then face high and tilted up, then again waist high, along the line. "Let's not get into anything, Lane. We have the girls with us."

"But they're celebrating his death." Lane tried to convince Frank.

Frank waited, then answered that he had always believed the President popular among the people of that country.

"You're all acting stupidly. I thought you had more sense than to get into a common street fight, Lane." Wendy dropped her cigaret, ground it between two cobblestones with her toe, and started walking up the block. Cleurdia hurried after her.

"Come on, honey." Marian hugged Ira's arm, pulled him away. "Wendy's right."

Lane shrugged. "We have better things to do anyway."

They began to walk again. A block ahead, the overpass, a section of Roman viaduct, straddled the narrow street. Just beyond the overpass waited the café. But now the natives marched after them, three in the front rank, two in the second. The native with the hamster's face, between two Jualoreursos, carried the bottle.

Wendy reached the overpass first. The arch's shadow closed around her—but soon the sun fired her yellow shorts and long legs.

Then she stopped, shrank back as if threatened, relaxed, and turned around to face them. Chig passed under the arch last. Just on the far side, he discovered two figures in brown uniforms, crouched behind the pillars, policemen.

When Chig had passed, the policemen stepped into the center of the street, executed quarter-turns to face the natives.

"Halt. Hand us your identities." They started forward, the backs of their brown tunics studded with gold buttons, trimmed with gold braid. Each policeman carried a smooth white club, three feet long. "Halt, I say!"

The natives stopped, patted themselves, mumbling. The

Atzuoreurso with the hamster's face put the bottle on the cobblestones. "Ask them for their identities, my sir. They have offended."

"Identities, my sir." The older policeman, tall, gray, his brown uniform frayed but neat, did the talking. "Is it that you do not realize that two of your number had chosen yellowredness and three blueredness?"

The older policeman's partner, tiny, tidy, his uniform new, stood beside him, his neck tensed into his brown wool shoulders, beating his thigh with his club.

"Their President has become killed. Tomorrow it will start war."

"Today, not tomorrow, we ask for your identities, my sir."

The Atzuoreurso balled his fist, opened his mouth, but the younger policeman, pouncing, stopped his voice, the knocking of his white club on the native's head swollen by the arch's echo. Soon, the native had sprawled to the cobblestones, the policeman over him, his brown arm rising, falling above the native's head, ribs, and knees.

The older policeman inspected their papers. "Now, my sirs, go to your houses. Your friend is in our care. And remember that all must abide the morning choice. The fate of the Eagle means no concern to you."

He returned their papers. Each native thanked him, nodded a good-bye to his friends and hurried back down the street, two Atzuoreursos on one sidewalk, two Jualoreursos on the other.

The policemen helped their prisoner to his feet, holding him away from their uniforms. They gave quick salutes to Chig and his friends, and started away.

"Wow." Chig watched after them. "The last time I saw something like that I was on my way home from school and—" He turned and realized his friends did not listen. They had almost reached the door of the Café of One Hand.

5

CHIG'S FRIENDS TOOK PLACES around a large rectangular table on the Jualoreurso side of the Café of One Hand. Lane had steered Cleurdia to the far side and into the corner, taking the middle chair for himself. Ira sat next to him on one of the aisle chairs, across from Marian. Wendy faced Cleurdia, her black hair partly covering the back of her chair. Frank sat at the end of the table, in the aisle.

A vacant chair waited between Wendy and Marian. "Here's a place for you, Chig. I saved it. Right here. Sit down."

He waited for Marian to stop slapping the dark brittle wood, then sat down. The tiny policeman had moved so fast. "Did you see that cop work out?"

"I keep my dealings with authorities to a minimum." Ira frowned. "Don't give him a chance to get his hand on you. Because once he gets you, we're all the same. After he arrests you, the only thing that matters is that you're a captive and he's a captor. That's what my father says."

"Maybe it's that way in the big city, but out our way, we feel different about the police."

"There's another way to feel about the police, Lane?" Ira winked at Chig.

"You don't think, Ira. Maybe that's why you're a real great artist." Framed in his shaggy sandy hair, Lane's ears grew red. "I was raised up in a small-town kind of environment and one thing I learned is that police are people. In a small town you get to know a policeman. He has a wife and kids. My father grew up with the sheriff in our town. He started deputy around the time my father went up to State. I knew him all my life. When I got to be a senior in Prairie Park High, I used to ride around in his patrol car. Saturday nights. Sometimes they'd call him, some trouble in the Pit. A cutting or something. Blood all over the place, loud music on the jukebox, a big ugly mess. And I'd go with him. He wasn't just a policeman. He tried to help other people. We used to have a good time, me and Uncle Jorry Burrell."

Ira shrugged. "Well, maybe you're right about small-town life. But in the city you're just lost."

"Lots of lonely lovers in the city." Marian nodded, quoting something. "Everyone's looking for a hole to crawl into where they'll say you're home."

Lane stared across the table for a moment. "What's the time, Frank?"

"Three-forty."

"No wonder I'm so hungry." He leaned back, rounded out his chest and stomach, slapped himself with both hands. "I'm eating."

"I'm hungry too." Frank twisted in his seat, looking for the Jualoreurso waiter. Divided in two by the center aisle, each side of the café received service from a waiter wearing the proper-colored vest.

The Jualoreurso waiter, a fat little man with dark hair

watered flat, combed back, unparted, greeted them with a shrug of soft narrow shoulders. "My sirs, forgive. Forgive. What can this man say? Forgive."

"Now, what's he trying to sell? Get me a menu, will you, Frank?"

The waiter blinked, went on. "Is it that you have a revolution in your birthland? Forgive me to ask." He shook his head.

"Did he have a kid?" Lane pinched Cleurdia's arm. "He didn't want it, huh?"

"He is asking Frank about the revolution in your country."

"What?"

". . . whose uncle, at this time current, living in the New Hershey. The day he departed, saying, I read the books historical. Fifty-five years without revolution, a land of peace. I have say him, one day, same as all men. That was in the year one thousand nine hundred twenty. It is not pleasing to me that I am right." He held a pale yellow dishtowel, twisted it to rope.

"There is no revolution," Frank answered. "But if it becomes the slightest possibility that the Commonist has done it, it will bring the war possible."

"Tell him he was wrong, Frank. In 1920, it was a hundred thirty-one years since the Revolution."

"But, my sirs, I am he and we had having the profound respect for your President. We regarded him an aristocrat with sympathy for the poor, the kindly tyrant."

"You see, Lane?" Frank wagged his finger. "That's what I told you before."

"He said he was on the other side, didn't he?"

Frank turned back to the waiter. "If the Commonist have not kill him, in that case, who has done it?"

"Is it that you do not collect information in your affairs national?" The waiter raised his eyebrows, snapped the wrinkles from his towel. "The journal late of the Commonist has reported that he loved to nationalize the industry of metallics." He waited for an answer, received none, took advantage of the silence to fetch their menus. He dropped them on the table and scurried away to a family in canvassy yellow cardigan jackets, a husband and wife, two small red-haired girls.

"What did he say?" Lane took a menu, opened it on the table between Cleurdia and himself.

"What do you want, Ira?" Marian's menu rested on her breasts. "Why don't you have . . . wait, I lost it."

"He said the President was going to nationalize steel." Frank looked around the table. "I never heard that before."

"Have you ever tried the veal and bacon here, Chig?" Wendy shifted in her place, moving her thigh against his. She did not seem aware of it. "It's very good."

He realized that his mouth hung open, closed it, trying to think of his answer.

"I want beef stew and potatoes." Lane came up from his menu. "Reason you never heard it, Frank, is because no President would dare do that. The Roomp was lying, or spreading a lie he read in some little mimeographed sheet."

Chig and his friends nodded, agreeing. Of course, the Commonists filled their paper with lies. "But he did make Frank's point. The other side respected him. The President."

"They used him, Chig. But they never respected him. When he wasn't useful anymore, they disposed of him."

"That's not true, Lane." Frank seemed deeply insulted. "He was his own man."

"His own man, huh? What about . . . Just forget it."

"You always do that, Lane. You start something and then let it drop. What about when? Go on, tell me."

Lane had stopped listening. He put his arm around Cleurdia's shoulder, whispered into her ear, then gave her neck a little kiss. Her face remained still.

Frank appealed to Ira. "You see that? He never finishes his thought."

"He's busy." Ira smiled. "Come back after lunch."

Chig and Marian laughed; Frank smiled. He still had blood on his upper lip, and brown polka-dots of blood spotted his yellow ascot.

The waiter returned, a homemade pad of torn wrapping-paper in his hand, and took their orders. They all started with thick, black bean soup. After the soup, Wendy had ordered veal and bacon, with a small dish of a leafy, chewy vegetable seasoned with vinegar. Marian convinced Ira they both should have chicken spiced with marjoram, and potatoes. Cleurdia ate fish stuffed with cheese. As he had announced earlier, Lane got beef stew and potatoes. Frank, with a longing glance Cleurdia's way, asked for fish stuffed with cheese. Chig ordered just after Wendy, echoed her. She did not smile.

It did not bother him. He knew, despite their friends' liberal attitudes, it would be difficult for her to take the step of liking him, or even to show she considered it. In public, he expected no concrete sign. But he believed he had made progress. He enjoyed the meal Wendy had chosen. Finished, he leaned back in his chair, nicely dazed with food and dark red wine, and watched Frank spoon onto his plate the last of the beef stew Lane had ordered.

"Okay, Lane?" Frank crossed his arms, steam from the stew rising to his raised chin. "Is that okay? You don't mind me finishing your stew, do you?"

"No, Frank." He paused. "But I thought you weren't supposed to eat meat on Sunday."

"That's Friday, and—"

"Oh, I thought it was Sunday."

"It is Sunday, Lane," Ira commented. "Just another working day."

Marian and Chig laughed.

Frank ignored them. "Just as long as you don't mind me finishing your stew." He held a chunk of meat on his fork. "And, by the way, did you come up with that date yet?"

Lane looked up from his plate. "Date?"

"Yes, you were about to tell me the date the other side used the President." He ate the meat-chunk. "The late President."

"No, I was not. That's what you thought I'd do." Lane popped a potato into his mouth, continued: "Much, much more sophisticated than that." He swallowed. "People guide you and you don't even know it. You don't have simple traitors anymore like Benedict Arnold."

"How can you talk about them in the same context? One was a general, and—"

"I lump them together because each in his own way, Frank, remember that, each in his own way, let his country down." He waved his hand in Frank's face. "Wittingly or unwittingly. His pattern shows what he was. The things he did all along the line. As if he was driven to it, destined to do it." He shook his head. "That's the thing, Frank. I'm not saying he meant to be a traitor. Maybe he honestly thought he was doing the right thing."

"That's just not true." When he got excited, Frank's voice went high, but not squeaky. "His actions showed he had a vision of the future. And I'm sure he always had a moral base for what he did."

"I'm not talking about morals, Frank. That's a personal thing. Moral base means nothing." He looked around the table for something more to eat. "His life forms an immoral pattern, if you want to get over into that area. But that's because it's very sophisticated now. It's not simple anymore, like, say, Pontius

Pilate." He picked up a spoon and began to scrape the last of fish stuffed with cheese onto his plate. "You understand now?"

"That's not fair. In the first place, we have no doubts that Pilate knew he was doing wrong because he washed his hands. Lane, are you listening?" He looked down at Lane's head. "Hey, that's my cheese-in-fish."

"No, it isn't." Lane did not raise his head. "It's Cloode's."

"Wait a minute, Lane. Cleurdia and I were supposed to share that platter."

"You had yours. Besides, you made a hog of yourself with my stew."

"You said it was all right. I only had one helping of cheese-in-fish. I have seconds coming."

"Listen, I saw you gulp down at least three servings." He chewed as he talked.

"Three?"

"You see that?" Lane turned to Cleurdia. "He's trying to hog your cheese-in-fish."

"That's not true!" Frank sat up straight. "It's the principle."

Lane fingered the hair away from Cleurdia's ear, whispered to her. Quite suddenly, she laughed, once. Lane continued to whisper.

"Lane? Lane? Lane, listen. Lane?"

"Frank, for golly's sake, I'm trying to tell her something."

"What about my cheese-in-fish?"

"Oh, take your cheese-in-fish . . ." He picked up his plate and extended it toward Frank. But before Frank could raise his hands to receive it, Lane let go.

"You did that on purpose, Lane." Kicking his chair back into the aisle, Frank rose to his feet, and started around the table, his arms raised. "You did that on purpose."

Lane met him, ducked Frank's embrace and pushed him off-balance, and onto Ira. The table jumped, skidded.

"You see, Frank? Look!" Lane stood over the kneeling Frank. "Look at what you did to Chig's pants, you stupid shit!"

Dark, red wine had dyed the lap of Chig's yellow pants.

"What I did? It wasn't just my fault, Lane." Frank stood up, came around the table, his head lowered. "Lane and I'll pay for the cleaning, Chig."

They all made a fuss over Chig's pants. They hoped the pants could be cleaned, felt sure they could be. But Chig knew already that the dark stain would never disappear.

6

OLEURBA LUA FONTA DOL VOLADRO
AVCON O SABEURL!
(Up the well of the thief with a sword!)

> Mona Cono sells the best fish.
> Free Delivery. Call 63.39.93

If the soft ones spout hard,
and the hard ones spout soft,
there would be no jealousy,
and thus,
no War.

> Expert carpenter
> has BUILT
> many boxes.
> UP early, call after 9.
> 38.76.40

See what happened? And I have a date with a Gerd.

Buy Yellowredness!   DOWN
            WITH
            THE
            NOSE!

Continue the struggle after the explosion!

He stood reading in the toilet room of the Café of One Hand, a cubicle with a fist-sized hole in the middle of its white tile floor. The corner's sink, one spigot, cold, dripped. Like most public toilets Chig had ever used, writings covered the walls.

The stain had almost dried, but Chig dawdled, troubled by his feelings. At the table, he had begun to sweat with the realization that he neither loved nor hated the late President. The man had seemed capable enough, a little more honest and sincere than most politicians. But these qualities had not produced in Chig the feelings that boiled inside his friends. The man remained, quite simply, an ordinary President.

He knew he could not stay away from his friends for more than a few minutes; they would think his ruined pants upset him. He used only water on his hands, dried them with toilet-paper, then unlocked the door.

"God Chig, I'm about to bust!" Marian waited outside in the hallway. "Your pants all right?"

He nodded, held the door for her.

She slipped by him. "Wait for me, Chig. I want to ask you something about Lane." She closed the door on her smile.

He leaned against the hallway wall, looking out into the café. In the center aisle, an Atzuoreurso, very drunk, danced, a glass of wine balanced on his forehead. He looked at the ceiling and spun in circles, his face and collar covered with wine while the Atzuoreursos applauded him. When the glass on his head had emptied, he sat down, and began to cry.

Marian unlocked the door and stepped into the hallway. "I dread that place. No wonder so many of them get bad kidneys. And it's worse for a girl because we have to squat."

He could not think of a comment, then remembered why she had asked him to wait. "What about Lane?"

"What?" She half-closed her eyes. "About Lane?"

"You had some gossip." He often kidded her about gossiping. They all gossiped.

"No, I don't, Chig. It's just that Lane, well, you know Lane."

He did not understand.

"He, you know, he was getting real sexy with Cleurdia, right in front of us. You don't think that's right, do you?"

"I don't guess not." He shook his head, hoping she would not ask him to talk to Lane. He had acted as a messenger for his friends more than once. If Frank wanted Ira to know something, but could not tell him, he asked Chig to carry the message. He had conveyed messages from Cleurdia to Lane, Lane to Ira, Ira to Lane, Marian to Frank, Frank to Cleurdia. Only Wendy had never used him as a messenger.

"But to feel her up like that. Today especially."

"When today?"

"After you left."

"What did she say?"

"What could she say?"

He shrugged. "She should say something. I mean, we can't do anything unless she complains." He smiled. "She might even enjoy it."

"That's cruel, Chig." She lowered her chin, but kept her eyes on his. "She doesn't know what's going on most of the time. Someone should really say something to him."

"Maybe so."

"You know what he did after you left the table? He grabbed her breast, like this." She reached for him. "He didn't just pinch it, like that, he just kind of squeezed it a few times." She did not remove her hand from his chest. "Today of all days, with the President dead like that. He shouldn't be acting like that. Something might really be wrong in the country and we might all have to go back. What if they find out the people who killed him are Southerners? The Negroes might revolt to avenge his

death. We'd have to do something. It's our country and we'd
have to save it."

She moved closer as she talked, her hand caught in the trap
formed by her breasts and his chest. She looked up at him, concern in her eyes. "There was hope with him. And now it's different. I know the country's in good hands, but they're not the
same hands."

She pressed him to the wall; she seemed boneless. "Especially after how he died. The pictures'll be horrible, lots of
blood, closeups. Oh, it's so disgusting." One tear started out of
each eye; she rested her forehead against his collarbone. "You
have real strength, Chig. You inspire me. I'm an artist and
that means I have bad moods, but you never seem to worry
about anything. I mean, you should be really bitter and hate-
filled, but you're always so sweet and strong. I hope I can keep
myself sweet if my art isn't recognized or something like that."
She kissed him on the cheek, put her arms around his waist,
hugged him tightly, then pushed him away. "Chig, you have a
hard-on."

He could not deny it. "Well, really Marian, you shouldn't,
you know, hug me." He laughed. "I mean, you must know
you're, well, sexy—"

"You mean you think I'm trying to make you?"

"I didn't mean that, Marian. I know you love Ira, but—"

"Then why did you get like that?" She pointed at the wine
stain.

"I couldn't help it, Marian."

"You couldn't help it? God, what's wrong with you? One
hug and you act like I'm raping you? God."

"Wait a minute, Marian." It surprised him to discover his
anger building. "I didn't accuse you of anything. But I wish,
well, you wouldn't rub up against me. You are—"

"Me? I'm not doing anything but trying to be nice. I just

want to show you that I like you. As an ordinary person. Can't you accept that? You act like I'm doing something dirty."

He smiled. "I didn't say it was dirty. Just disturbing."

She put her hands on her hips. "God, Chig, you're over-sexed. And don't think I haven't noticed it before. You didn't have to tell me you think I'm sexy. I know already how you feel about me. You just be glad I don't tell Ira, whose friend you're supposed to be. But every time I turn around, there you are. At first it was flattering, but now you stick that hard-on into my stomach. God! And Ira thinks you're his friend. Talk about me? You're the one who's always raping me. And you think I'm stupid and don't know it." She started away, then stopped, returned. "Today of all days. You must have some high opinion of yourself. You must really think you're sexier than ordinary people. Well, I don't. But if you want to believe that, go on. I'm just warning you, Chig, the next time, I'll tell Ira."

He watched her return to their table and sit down, in his chair. His friends ignored her. They had ordered a new bottle of wine, had consumed half of it. Ira leaned over his glass, rocking forward and back. Frank lectured Lane, who did not listen. He had busied himself with snapping the strap of Cleurdia's bras-siere. In the corner, Wendy smoked. Then over the heads of his friends, she looked at him, and he thought that she smiled an instant.

On impulse, he winked.

Back winked one dark brown eye.

7

HE RETURNED TO THE TABLE and sat next to Marian.

Frank talked on: ". . . about the way the branches of the government balance that no one else ever solved before. In the Judiciary, we have nine men who sit above politics." He counted on stiff fingers. "In the Legislature, the direct representatives of small groups of common people, and regional representation too. And in the Administrative, a man elected by all the people—"

"So what took you so long, Chig?" Ira raised his head, stopped rocking, sipped his wine. "Marian talk your ear in?"

Frank snorted.

"In a way, Ira." He smiled. "She warned me against my worst enemy. Isn't that right, Marian?"

"Yes." She tried to laugh. "I warned him."

"Against who, Chigboy?"

"My enemy."

"I sure hope it's nobody here."

Chig almost asked Lane why he hoped that, then decided to let the matter die. "Nobody here now."

"Good, and so back to the wooing of Cloode." He laughed, leaned down and kissed Cleurdia's breast, leaving wet lip marks on her pink cotton blouse. "I'm getting hitched and taking her back with me."

"All that happen while I was in the W.C.?" His mouth tasted vinegar, excitement left over perhaps from his encounter with Marian. His mind buzzed.

"Yes sirree, Mr. Dunford, while you were in the old W.C." Cleurdia's bra snapped. She sat quietly, her hands in her lap, her face a face in a portrait in a museum.

Chig smiled. "Who's best man?"

"Well, Ira seems prejudiced against marriage, and Frank's church won't let him inside mine . . ."

"That's not true, Lane."

". . . so that leaves you. Okay?"

"It'll be a pleasure." He reached for the bottle. "Let's drink to it."

"That's a good idea." Lane pushed forward his glass. "Damn good idea. Huh, Cloode?"

"Yes, Lane."

Chig filled all their glasses, put the bottle down.

"We're drinking to my wedding, right?"

"Just about." Chig clinked Lane's glass. They drank.

"My fellow countrymen, and you too Cloode, I guess wine in the afternoon is getting to me a little bit, but I'm listening." Lane began to talk. "I'm listening to you, Frank, and you're right. It's really great to come from a country like ours. Every four years, like in spring, the people have their say. And it runs so smooth we all just take it for granted. But I bet Cloode understands what I'm saying. This country's a mess." He leaned on Cleurdia, his hands beneath the table. She blushed. "Don't you, honeybunch?"

"Yes, Lane."

"That's the thing we should remember, specially today. Presidents come and go, but the government continues on. We should drink to that." He picked up the bottle, emptied it into their glasses. "I want to propose another toast. I'm not afraid to wave a flag sometimes, even if painters are supposed to be cynical." He lifted his glass. "To home."

Frank nodded. "Sure."

"No matter what my father says it's certainly the best place in the world to be an artist." Ira clicked glasses with Frank, then Lane. "At least some bureaucrat isn't telling you what—"

". . . the government is to somebody else's and you'll see just how true what I just said is. It's the best civilized man has developed, better than the Greeks even."

Cleurdia raised her glass, her hand shaking. Marian stopped brooding to join the toast. Wendy held her glass a few inches from her tanned cheek, disinterested. Chig imitated her. Then they drained their glasses, and quietly at first Lane started singing, one of the two or three songs the people back home considered patriotic:

God, our Father, gave this country . . .

First Frank, then Wendy began to sing with him.

Hills of iron and oak trees wintry . . .

Ira and Marian came in, smiling at each other. Even Cleurdia hummed.

To be a place of liberty . . .

But Chig could not remember the words. He looked at their mouths, trying to read their lips.

Pilgrims bold brought faith of old . . .
To start anew in the wilderness cold . . .
A place for liberty to ring!

"What's wrong with you?" Lane leaned on his elbows, staring at him.

"I was listening."

"Listening?" He turned to Frank. "You hear that?"

Frank lowered his eyes. The rest looked at him.

"Well, didn't you feel like singing?"

He could only smile; his mind still buzzed, louder now.

"Chigboy, did you hear me? Didn't you feel—"

"No, motherfucker!" Wow.

Lane's face grew very white, then very red. Chig waited for more to happen.

"Marian?" Ira struggled to his feet. "I think I'm going to work today, maybe an homage to a fallen President. Anybody take a lift?"

"I will." Wendy mashed out her cigaret.

Chig stood up; Marian, then Wendy came out into the aisle, avoiding his eyes.

"Come on." Lane got up. "Me and Cloode are going to spend a nice Sunday evening at my place."

"I guess you can drop me off, Ira." For the day at least, Frank had lost her.

They all nodded good-bye, but no one spoke.

Chig sat down, in the corner, in Wendy's place. Clean white butts filled the ashtray on the table in front of him. She did not wear lipstick. He guessed he had upset her; she had left so quickly. Where on earth had those words come from? He tried always to choose his words with care, to hold back even anger until he found the correct words. Luckily, he had never suffered a pronunciation problem. His family lived in Harlem; he had grown up there, but had no trouble saying that, they, these, those or them. He had always spoken properly at Shaddy Bend Primary School. There, he had never heard those words, and as a gradeschooler, one of his parents had always driven him to school and back. But when he continued on to Shaddy Bend Upper School, twice each weekday he had walked between his house and the subway. Some days he had stopped to watch boys playing in the street, had heard that kind of talk, must have remembered it. He smiled, laughed behind closed lips, at the street words that had waited inside him all these years to jump out at Lane's face. He shook his head, resigned. He would always stay—

"Chig, I told them I lost my lighter." Wendy stood at the end of the table. "Do you know my phone number?"

"Yes, Wendy."

"Please call me tomorrow." She turned and walked toward the door, the long black hair around her ears catching in a breeze, tanned cheeks glowing in the late-day light of the café.

He half-rose, nodded at her back, to himself, whispering, "I will, Wendy."

Maya we now go on wi yReconstruction, Mr. Chuggle? Awick now?

8

WITCHES ONE WAY tspike Mr. Chigyle's Languish, n curryng him back tRealty, recoremince wi hUnmisereaducation. Maya we now go on wi yReconstruction, Mr. Chuggle? Awick now? Goodd, a'god Moanng agen everybubbahs n babys among you, d'yonLadys in front who always come vear too, days ago, dhisMorning we wddeal, in dhis Sagmint of Lecturian Angleash 161, w'all the daisiastrous effects, the foxnoxious bland of stimili, the infortunelessnesses of circusdances which weak to worsen the phistorystematical intrafricanical firmly structure of our distinct coresins: The Blafringro-Arumericans.

Highever, in the meantime, with diwrect concern to Mr. Chigstyle's dreamage (C. Fraud, moufetitis), the New Africurekey Univercity Family have receive nouzelle of the missaltoetumble of the leader of La Colon y de la Thour Yndia Company, Prestodent Eurchill Balderman, preachful as expected, L. Oki to fry.

But list we lest ourselfs sin sorroifall exortations, rowmember these Iklanders have profistyed it all before tomera. It wire in the gerdle of the udder muddercow who liked the case of ice and landed under Yan Mira's heed. Her, she came; the air she knows that he vile vraise.

Suppositively! He always do. To get musseldeaded aginning with each spring and coil of his guiltilokiting hide. But that anether world, an ackackcident, ache you. N'Arreterre, Pass!

Now hoose wandering about his sweetarte? You Mr. Cargole? Can't make any cents of her mirther? Issue asking ifit a real or state cryme? Wender who's kissing there now?

Siriously, why you barbed in his woofe? You shoelacily know that's dangleous tintering. It keys us lowkeyed up.

There be an old Dheysaypian proverb which titches: A fool will pour ant ox with uncle elephant. Preciously the pwant, for, three two one of the reasons that some peoplee common called Theuroman in the political until within question, sum of the reasons some Useuropeans fight the antigrition of the Afriman, comingly called Neargrows, but actually Afrikins attending, into the sauciety is because some think we only won't the Ire women, pink and licey, to dove them, deary them, dive them, or dumpthin or druther; whil efew eisllion others don't care too much abat that, there so high up, slaying things like: give a gillion of that, and one only little shiny, Brightdear—and don't have to worry about just any cadillacquered pushpoy.

But those oather that think that that's what we want, he were a very surprisingly unexpected one to encounter in our sojoin amung them. He seem not to know that the majority of them simmer to haunt us to hilt their hair-billowing bunides, to top the tip of the rolled back a round of cream on the face, to lighten up, tote that bore, straight that head, and nig that woman.

His fright is with Major I. T. Hardboild, stars on his sleeve, greece in his hair. Or why else start the stellavision and see all legs and six whide inches deep, blacknetted, spangled bhunners.

Tits a playsure to be her, Jerky. I'm opening my self at the Scissor Room.

Runold, Reena's been rupted.

Here she is, fox, Miss Armourinco, tongue to teeth, tears immi ice, Mamamammary Mamungro.

Are we cursens, brooders, shestirs, zuncles, antes, Poos, and Moos supposed to look at all that sawfat, butter to spread than any cheapy, and utter:

Owndy? Compair this Sapphire to that Furd's dullall exhaust. Shufire came along, hard way, cruising and maid to crew, in the dues, singing, with a camel in her heat combed or not—what dew it really cure?—pecked cotton and all such mathers, with you, tried men and exitcuted for you.

War as, look at Mist Blue Cheeseknees, their champoiness, mussoming down her dress, and limping over, Long Joan Sliver, rogerbone crusted and skulled, ready to dip a dagger into your hurt.

Know! Who would want us not to loafer? At least it seams sew at needless point. That is why this Useropean will give a throttle when we meet him. His eyes arout of trot with his silocal freyrners.

Ivyn from the plant of fiew of the undividual, the avaridge hiceman don't seem uphupset which another man pays even friendishly ittension to his wife. He, who feel prodove his vive seem eased to hear good things about her spreeformancers. He loves tubby claplimented abort her:

Wee had a lusterly time whizz that wuman of yearn lost knight.

I've sin pitches ova, but chaise bitter in the flush.

Your wife certainly is a fun cooker.

Of coitse, no man wants any herm to troyble his wife in anal-ley way. He wants to keep her from Hummin or any outer bun with a shiggy face on it, and a slit your bladder cutslass in his picket, chanting ur spooking Snigger, Barrion, or even Kiteski. But that sirtainly should robber a man not, as long as he knows her ass safe as sealed. For in the other hand, would he want to get the infirmation his wife is mightly muggly, pimplepacked, a pink peel of bill, like in slumways, a parrotute.

We can agree then that a Useupian looks similair to us and thee, be proud of his woman. So din what's the big dill? Why get so upchut when a tinny, minny binch of a bunch of bagheaded neergrows show any nosense suchly, beginning to buy what's been standing fursolong in the gate, ready to run like a washingpotomatic muxing vowel, with two springers, just the laitest from Frinch and Angles on Filthy-servanth Street in Niew Yoke City?

Some Usricans say it's because the Uralpean ist d'DeVille. They razen He'll tempt you, tissyue, tuss you, tighten your truest with gleeven, his Job, as illmost any quistian will taile you. And when in disoughther, you ardor: Say, Mistear Blanchemchiller, rip arind dhat oven witch the chat on chanel 992,828,296,645 (p73,78,6,68: Bla Ckcat Dreambo, OK?) havidvertized. And make surashitit have two top adjerkable burners to light my way into deArk, past the Oreman, pissed Otissender, and into that kitshunned, closeted, clotted, cloistered corset at the Doorset. I'm ready to cook! I'm ready to riddle them pants and pit. I'm hangling the hardiest piece of jamon! Earth, I'm holding the pertiest beninsular into the Bay of Barburbia that the four granyteheads on Mount Yowomenn have over beheld. And I'm re-eddy! Here ism eye sad dress—

Up Pops! His Histewichill Majosty, Natas The Lived, gleaming white heat, tail flapping, his trustee trepicoed pinter pointed at your penals, and in one hand, the bigotest, banjodist, boosterist shotgunghadin your bruised blackeyes have ever seen!

But the blew vue seems sinnicle, and to a large exscent, defffutilest. To say that the Usepin is deFils is the sum of saying the pretoperticular poisons we discuss are superhumain, a soupupper whirling birdyplane smowing down deseased slingtied moogeymen with the fleakpower of his merchantize.

No thank you, Mastur and Mistris Chillerman, we'll take you humus, and humbagless. Humas you air, and hummingless you remain furrover.

The questjung reminds still. Why, when those off us that gwhine that way, run up Hattanhand, waving aside Malma-Mae to buy boy bye the bearettes—why do skiers flie and fists flight? How do the tampors at Camp Tiwayo get out the shatgrins and flupipointed hats? When do the balls gangle over the palmbreaker's bedpost? Why such constarenation?

E. M. Fardpull, in his landark steady of the study hobits of the eurly tribs of the eorly Yacuvic Pyreod, THE MESS AGE OF THE LACKMAN, states clearly his bilefe in the thory of mismagination and expelcion, the eeveel reck of the hubristic Jack L. Yacoo, M.D.

But yours trolley huffling professanityr, wool not covering his eyes to the identicuality of doubtcome, can see a clare noncoilition between the lacke of the sun and the luck of the pepills on that spand of Terrifyrma, both in the Furtherland and the Motorcoloniel, glacerfied as the Outterre Wreckwitorial Bolt.

The sun beaming the source of all emcergy hit your big, blrown Mamal's tights and heirs and bolleys and moleteins most evory afternoun around the pool at the Lake Vik Hotel. There you got your birthbin. There she dalied, darkened by day, greener dang rain, hohannesbig at the rounded buttem, bowed at the bubberia, pinched in the reygion of her tawny stembuck too. You couldn't wait to git a.m. from school to lay widher. You couldn't wait to get the homme to skul so you could run in the strait for her expression in flesh; which deskription inner mind, in contraced to the Momhoo hauting the rocker on the northside of Mudderterrorhanian Ave., N.E.W., bids fire to apall.

Where have the skyheight go? Where have Miss Sunny Rod

*The Two Continents of the Outterre Wreckwitorial Bolt, and New
Afriquequerque*

Hidinghod and her basket run? Oh son unsown why haven you
foresuckered them? we may writfully ax. Daddybaddy what
did you deed: little meanimum scirrel from pit to pid; whittle
nittle nam nip frim din til dip. Traygic. Period. Its cold; tits
cold; sheets cauld run me the noose drops, please. Notenough
bush on hand to blow a burgle downly; not aknife spice on ice
to fill a sport. Studium!

Whabout warsir?

Absoakutely correct, Mr. Chaca. The afurormentioned
cainstirnation gets us used for fuil where you find a followar
of W. Oten-Chiltman, Profursir Ymiratus, Cornwhales, who
fund a way to suppertute Raw actiwity in liw of Nus nummora-
bility by piking a pole with a pwinted stock into a pic to peal his
pouch, to light a Londamn fire. It war him totem to cain a buy,
and punt a balder in forty pounlbs of mail-odor maiseplated
amour to warm the ashes on the strangler's high-chair. It ware
him wired them to turn onto a bearserk and bury a hammer

into the noirl of a fang. Almist since the bin of bawn, he lobbed them to lobe a heart for the frigg of it, unrevel a ball for the yarn of it, barn a burn for the beef of it, but a hut for the strut of it, incise a shoe for the sock of it, heat a sheat for the wick of it. That and Alotoflikkyr and Heshappy, Mr. Chilyle.

Dewar's Den be the sette where his bludgeon redheaded, height and blue?

You beat your swif tunwon ass and it will his tomorrow a world of Hammobiles!

9

ALL HUES IN PARTICOLOR, Mr. Chiglyle.

But Priministir Shill, his elf Hinch, and their huff cannot belawd to monsterize our discaution. Waterboat the fymale Oiccidental?

Mum, toillustrate the why Mrs. Iadlebody Shrillorsolf eels around the manor, house about tuning over to the chase of un humble iceflown furwestered Afterchain: Uncle Turtom, living but wearyking in a sircurse, a lowlisweeperepper in behind of a fartaphant.

We journ auxld Tum (so-collared) one day shawtly afta what, if we be lengleashtically corerect we must call the Second Intergenerational Untralingustic Antirepublican Cunfronta- tion. We find him subbing and watshing his foolaphant, tink- ing with the idya of putting roast shocks in a box and selling two for one fantastickly new punnut, when his bosstoiler, the Hun. Hans Dan Shillisif, Executionerative Prosistant of the Rundawirlde, Grabapease & Bargin M. Fytine Sircoarse, hat- pinned up in a blue threebuttoned, tattercolored sweat. It some like Addlebabby, a onetime exactobat at biending her long legs behind her neck while suxpanded on a rope of the hair just over her braud and puckered forebrain above the heads of the maltitudes, since his reburnth from the Ward wiern't eeble to steeple to the top of the tent on his type; there to oversee the soose, peck the piwint, surround an arrow in a quivvver.

Moister didn't toyn her roiled roind anymower. So it came tame to seek Taim, the bugshow's shootscooper, acksing ofoam the whyfore of his wumbfinder, to answer the riddle of Addlebody's ditole, His Horner, Moster Shail having noticed that no suuner than the son shipped under the whoreyesin, and old Tim Aritan soaped off that oriphant's hat that the aged racooner wasasswarm with a hirem of maalmiable addmyras, Betty-Suthan Herchile one among them, in grin shorts slit to her choco-covered ribs, and a halter hitching up her hi dibble dOOples.

Of case, Mesiter Prudident didn't come moot with his probelimb, but ruder, patted Tamovar the head, and crooked his mouth into a grim:

Tum, my sleighve, how's the faminely? Your Arnt Maeda, when I was a baiboy, used to rocka me on her bossem like my owned mammy. I met your old Conacrease-boat bringing her from the messionfaries, who salted her precaged in porkiron, a Bipple under her harm. She nellied at my tyred old mother's dedside at the morment she passed wind-ding over the Greet Dividered in a wooden coffired wagon of decompassed eilness. Maeda, when she was but a wee bit tight, tended my further the currnhell, who filt gravely sick after one of the slowves, a wappot, feygot to warn him the tdyme the Whoute Houske caught aphyre. Phaith-fyllid and eva, Maeda she feel?

Fined. Owe years, those were god dies for ebonybody. We used the sleep of the mighteous, nhiver reaching for depistle tucked unfriared under the pea-low's ear. Hyde hichup my bogey, two Arraybian stoolions spyking Sworehili pilling it,

Uncle Turtom, living but wearyking in a sircurse, a loulisweeperepper in behind of a fartaphant.

and raid out to see my biggers singing spurituals in the caugh-tom fields. And a shappier bunch of laboratoratatives have been never seen by any onionshop stuard! How could a goodies work hurt any Toddy? They knew horwell off they wise. Idlelady and me, us trulelie'd bought them interr the light. We sivved yum from the salvagery conseeyouming Puert Africo, given the grieft of servilization. You were hopi, whittle you, as pies in a stomach, as stew in a spit, as tomintow juiws in a bloody merrygoryund!

Ton listoned, the bogust smile on his fez that any sudden coloniel could club for. Do you gnaw what he snowing, Mr. Chigold? Do you know the weepon of the week? Let those with whippins more with pore, wile you, on bented skis llserve up arson eek! in scribbled eggs and puncakes, humberly mi ser, and put a possom pin in the collar that Mass wars.

His Majestority didn't see dot, but only stooped to inkwire: And watt've summer yawl din in reburn? Cost treble, ruining in the street disdrying pruberty wild we wharf viking the Bull's bowls. Open the Doily Paypoor and the herdlines make you chuke in your coughfee.

But not my olncle Tumoss, loi il etrue. The missiz rote often to tale how nurse you'd been when she got nurvus and all. Now she's umply and cratcheting. My bonus didn't even her out or hass her to or fro. She doesn't coo, or goo. Says it's me. Could it be? Want to see? Howie be? I till you, I'm in missouri and have to be showin. Pet me on a bed and tall me the ansir plus. Cus, shick, saint we all fellow broaders like Able and canine, or Robbingson Acreuso and his good fynd, Fidoy?

Buttom be one schooled in the users of sirsobience:

Pawn my soul, your horner, the hub he spoke, yam honored, postasentry soaruprized. The ringleader clumming to the rastabout a problim so puresonal. Let me stretch my gray mattered head for a mynut, but you realeyes I jester joker at heart, ain't in

the club, and on diamond, can only give a spyaid's advice, which
being going at a lady's bedy,

                              GO
                    down
          LEFT   den
                      pull
                      back-up
                      and
                      gosh down RIGHT
                      thin
                      pole
                      beak
                      and grouse
                      done
                      center
          ass   fore   ass
                      it cane
                      go
                      oo
                      !
                      !

Martial Shilichilf berried his peter, repeted Touchem's
unstucktions and wound round sarcas grounds (the dogface
boyked a gritting; the Samese fodlady, rumping with her twins,
miled wide) toward his holme, and Ladylbutty who waited
now abored a bed, silkimonoed, feet combing enrulered hair,
while hands hel Tomb, a noose, weakly.

But that wryunion war not to become a boutcause: Tollem's
faintafool, a recintipient of 1850 shuckerloafs, the gift of a child
or a man, had pulled up stake, and, a gnu whirld before his
ivory, had quomenced to question Macer Shechill's shimmy.

He was a true crushaider that felephont so nominal remanded encaged, not seal, or ailles, or cat or gnat or aardvlark or ox, the lastex beein a fleamale named Ouxley essie recall, and hide over hulls enemared of the elephun's horns from her first day admird them.

They ramparaded, that reimberserking evolutionary band, toring tent, detiring waygone, until that foolephant (every litre having a flow) humpened to pass Misory Shutchill's open wide oh to be, and glanzing in, unpocked his trunk, GONG to D-clef (muscically),

> to the riot,
>
> to
>
> the
>
> sent
>
> her
>
> too   Just like Tomboo!
>
> oo   oo
>
> oo   oo
>
> oo

Now, Mr. Charcycle, we reely see the itchuation. Star it. Take a nut. Under the bushkit always a brighthead! Behind a manger a manager! Bind an image and doubt squeezes a man, a swomen up the same stream, and he macks it because he must, mike no mystic about the lesson, Mr. Chairlyle.

How else could Tomisen play his tune, or tone his site? Could he be more imuman than anabama else? After sunset, on setty he too sits, eyessighted on his booxx, and loox, end-lessly upended, at Miss Aromarica's fweathered, dwithered, dimpilitoried eggs, her peatalled pushers, her posher pickle, her ploysure cooker, her ovarn, her pottled pipsicolon, her fugeted refoogerator (ice-o-meter open-tall), her transvestorized purt-able radiodor (Aim and Fem), her feeltered sugarets, her stern-less steel raisers, her parfoamed soup, her unpolstered funiture, her three-sperd stireo recurd chainger, her chronepleated, reun-forced bumperized, cheddaresisting wind-wipered, automanic, clutchriving carkiss. How could our Tomurai not sickcome?

But hear sermthing to take aholt on any dark Captuary night. Our fallenphant, please to notice, despirited though he mire've been, untiedied knot his Afriopian hurritage and had nadading to be dwing with that hornid ox.

10

Now will ox you, Mr. Chirlyle? Be your satisfreed from the dimage of the Muffitoy? Heave you learned your caughtomkidsm? Can we send you out on your hownor? Passable. But proveably not yetso tokentinue the cansolidation of the initiatory natsure of your helotionary sexperience, let we smiuve for illustration of chiltural rackage on the cause of a Hardlim denteeth who had stopped loving his wife. Before he stopped loving her, he had given her a wonderful wardrobe, a brownstone on the Hill, and a cottage on Long Island. Unfortunately, her appetite remained unappeased. She wanted one more thing—a cruise around the world. And so he asked her for a divorce.

She refused to give it to him.

He kept asking; she kept refusing. He began to feel trapped. He imagined himself cutting up her face, or pouring lye under each eyelid while she slept. He imagined ridding himself of her in many ways, but realized finally only one way lay open: he would have to catch her committing adultery.

Not that he felt certain she cheated on him. But he felt certain she might; after he stopped loving her, he had stopped making love to her. Common sense told him: if he was not between her legs, some other man could be.

But he could not catch her at it, and so decided to hire some man who would get under his wife's clothes and arrange to make pictures of the event.

Some man, named Carlyle Bedlow, sat in the dentist's chair (two small leather pillows messing his straightened hair) when the dentist made his proposal.

Carlyle's mind said Yes immediately, but he wanted to see if the dentist spoke seriously. He pretended reluctance, and also that such a job lay beneath him. "Man, you must be crazy. I don't do no shit like that." He pretended so well that, for a moment, he forgot the dentist had just pulled his tooth.

"You didn't let me finish." The dentist stood over him, Carlyle's molar clamped between the prongs of his silver pliers. He inspected the tooth, held it so Carlyle could look into its black hole. "You got to take better care of your mouth, Carlyle." He shook his head. "This tooth's a disgrace." He rested the pliers and the tooth in a metal dish. "Look, I'm in a spot and it's my only escape. Besides, I didn't mention money yet."

"You hurting me, man, so don't mention it. I don't go in for that kind of stuff." He specialized in smoke and warm fur coats.

The dentist pushed him deeper into his great chair, fingered his wound, and inserted fresh cotton between cheek and gum. "The blood's stopping." He smiled; the dentist himself knew a good dentist. "You realize this's legal? Got to be done by somebody and I'm just throwing the money your way. All you do: Take off her clothes, and have somebody to break in and take pictures."

"Why don't you ask her for a divorce?" He suspected that the dentist had done that.

"You think I didn't? And what you think she said? Yes?

Look, I'm in a prison with a crazy warden, trying to get me to do all kinds of crazy things." The dentist told Carlyle about his wife's obsession with sailing around the world.

Carlyle agreed; that did sound crazy, but he still pretended to hesitate. "Suppose she really don't got nobody else? Some women wait. I can think of at least one." Glora. "Besides, it ain't my thing."

"She hasn't waited. She's getting something somewhere. You don't understand how bad it is." He went to the glass door and opened it. "Mamie, come in here, will you, baby?"

Entering the office, hand against jaw, Carlyle had noticed Mamie's big, brown legs even through his pain. He had tried his smile on her, but her lips had not softened, had remained stretched across her teeth. Now she came in suspiciously, but smiled at the dentist after she closed the door.

"Meet my girl, Carlyle."

The pupils of her eyes looked black-brown. "Pleased to meet you."

"We want to get married." The dentist sat down. "And I thought you might help me out of friendship."

Carlyle nodded, leaned into the small basin beside him, and spat. He did not consider the dentist his friend. He did not even know the dentist's home phone number. Under arrest, he would not have wished to know it. They met, two or three times a month, by accident only, in Jack O'Gee's Golden Grouse Bar and Restaurant.

The dentist waited for Carlyle to straighten up before he continued. "Now I found me a sane woman, and can't live with that crazy one no more. I need those grounds!"

Carlyle glanced at Mamie to see if she had helped to plan the scheme. She leaned against the wall near the door, her face empty except for makeup, two shades lighter than her real skin. "How much you paying?"

"We ain't got no kids." The dentist hesitated; no kids formed part of the trouble. Carlyle had never married, but already had two children, visited their mothers when he had extra money. ". . . all going well, means no support. If I get her on adultery, I can cut the alimony down low. So it's worth a thousand if I get my pictures."

He had expected an offer of five hundred dollars, but did not tell that to the dentist. "Throw in my teeth."

The dentist agreed.

Carlyle climbed out of the dentist's leather chair. "Then I guess I'll turn legal for a while."

11

THEY AGREED TO MEET that night in the Grouse. The dentist would bring his wife. Carlyle would sit at their table. After that, they could only hope that the dentist's wife wanted another new man.

Carlyle stood at the bar over his second drink, when they came in. He had seen her only a few times before, and his memory had shown her kindness: she looked even less appetizing than he remembered her. She wore a dull pink dress that hung loosely from narrow shoulders, drowned high hard breasts and sharp-edged hips, her face the color of milk mixed with orange juice, the features squeezed into its center.

Passing by Carlyle on the way to the booths at the rear of the Grouse, the dentist did not speak or nod. But after helping his wife into a seat, and ordering her drink, he returned to the bar. "Bitch didn't want to come, but I told her I didn't want to stare at her all night."

Carlyle looked at the dentist's wife. She had already half-emptied the glass in front of her, a Brandy Alexander. "What happen to her when she drinking?"

"She cries."

Carlyle told the dentist the truth: "I like your money, but we'll never make it."

"Well, go ahead and try. One thousand dollars is a lot of money."

"You're right." He pushed away from the bar, leaving his drink, which had stung the dentist's work, and started toward the booth, the dentist close behind him.

She looked up at them, light-brown eyes in her light-orange face, but she did not speak.

"I haven't seen this man in years, Robena." The dentist suddenly pretended great excitement. "We served in the Army together." He introduced them.

Carlyle smiled. "Pleased to meet you." Her hand felt cold, filled with tiny bones.

"Have a seat." The dentist motioned him into the booth, next to his wife. As Carlyle settled himself, she finished her drink, pushed the foamed glass a few inches across the table.

"You want another?" She nodded; the dentist went on selling Carlyle. "We was in Asia. Right, Carlyle?"

"That's right." So far, Carlyle's luck had kept him from wearing any uniforms.

She looked at him now, seemed not to believe him.

"So how you been, Carlyle?" The dentist did not let him answer. "You do want another drink, don't you?"

She nodded, continuing to study Carlyle.

"What you been doing, man?"

"A little of a lot of things." He reached for his cigarets, wishing he had smoked for this meeting, trying to decide what to say if she wanted a more precise definition of his livelihood. But then she turned away.

The dentist did not give up. "Carlyle was a male nurse in the dental corps, even pulled some teeth when we had lots of work.

He was pretty good at it. I remember the first time I asked him to swing the hammer while I held the chisel. Cat's tooth broke off at the root." He started to laugh. "I had to keep telling Carlyle to hit harder. Finally got that sucker out though. Right, Carlyle?"

"That's right."

The waiter came with her drink. She drained half right away.

"She drinks that like lemonade, huh, Carlyle?"

He did not know what to answer. But he forced himself to speak, watching her eyes. "Some people take it better than others."

"And some get fallen down drunk."

She snorted, a short laugh, leaving Carlyle with a silence to fill. "Your wife don't look like that kind." He tried a broad smile.

"Yeah." The dentist finished his drink, put ten dollars on the table, and stood up. "I'll be right back." He went toward the restrooms, but when, fifteen minutes later, he had not returned, Carlyle realized the dentist had left him on his own.

Weather did not interest her, or Asia, or even hemlines. She would not speak, gave him no handle. When the ten dollar bill had dwindled to seven pennies and a dime, he helped her out of the booth, up the stairs to the street, and into a taxi.

On the Hill, she handed him a key and he opened the door. He stepped aside, knowing in this situation she would have to ask him inside. "Can you make it all right?"

She nodded, and started into the dark house with his thousand dollars. Then her heels stopped and turned back, but he could not see her pinched face. "You seem too smart to be his friend, Mr. Bedlow." She closed the door in his face.

12

THE NEXT DAY, Carlyle paid the dentist a visit. "Man, that was the wrongest thing you could've did, leaving like that. I got to sell myself under your nose."

Bent over his work table, the dentist inspected his tools. "What happened?"

"Nothing. She just filled up on that ten you left." He sat in the dentist's chair, and his jaw, remembering, began to throb. "We worse off than before."

"How you figure that?"

"Because now she connect me with a unhappy time. I got to have a chance to sympathize with her. But she didn't tell me nothing. I didn't ever get the chance to call you a bastard."

The dentist turned around, a small knife in his hand. "I couldn't sit there with that crazy bitch no more. I went to Mamie's."

"You have to hold that back if you want this to work. You educated and all, but you act dumb."

"I couldn't help it." He looked unhappy. "So you didn't make progress?"

"Nothing, man. As a matter of fact, I think she know we ain't army buddies, because at the end, she stuck her head out the door and tells me I'm too smart to be your friend—Mr. Bedlow."

"She did?" The dentist brightened. "God damn! You made it, Carlyle." He jumped, the knife shining in his fist. "Why didn't you tell me that before?"

Carlyle cleared his throat. "Remember you said you wanted to get out before you went crazy too?" He shook his head. "You too late."

"Listen." The dentist came toward him, waving the knife. "You're too smart to be my friend. That's a compliment."

Just then, Carlyle imagined himself sitting with a steady customer, selling a fur coat fresh from some unlocked car, perfume still strong in its silk lining. "She haven't mean a compliment. Not the way she said it."

"No, man. I know my wife. I'm a bad guy. But you're too smart to be my friend. She's going for it. Time for stage number two. The weekend's coming," he went on. Friday night, Carlyle, Mamie, the dentist and his wife would drive to the cottage at the end of Long Island. Mamie would go as Carlyle's date. But once they had arrived, Mamie and the dentist would have lots of paper work. Carlyle would seduce the dentist's wife. He felt so certain it would work that he told Carlyle to arrange to have someone ready to take pictures on Saturday night. He would put up the photographer at a small motel nearby.

Carlyle did not attempt to argue with him. He agreed to come to the office at six on Friday, with a suitcase full of attractive sports-clothes, the better to trap the dentist's wife.

13

THE DENTIST OWNED a very large automobile. Carlyle and Mamie—her big, beautiful thighs crossed—sat in the back. The dentist's wife stared out the open right-front window at cemeteries, airports, rows of pink and gray houses, and finally, sandy hills, covered with stubby Christmas trees and hard, dull-green bushes. Two hours from Harlem, they turned onto a dirt road. Then, even over the engine, Carlyle heard the music, as if they had made a giant circle, returning to the summer jukeboxes of the Avenue.

The community of cottages crowded in the dusk light around a small, bright bay. It did not look like Harlem, but if he had come on it by accident, Carlyle would have known that people of African descent lived there; by the music, the aroma of good food, barbecuing ribs, frying chickens. Carlyle had always believed that people like the dentist and his wife tried very hard to act European. If so, their music and food gave them away.

The dentist had built his glass and lacquered-wood house thirty yards from the beach. They sat around an empty yellow-brick fireplace, flicking their ashes into ceramic trays, while the dentist's wife fixed dinner. Behind her back, the dentist winked, smiled, waved at Mamie. Carlyle read a magazine, trying to give them privacy—and wondered if the dentist's wife actually did not know about Mamie and the dentist. They ate, drank two or three scotches apiece, tried to talk, and, at eleven, gave up and went to bed.

Carlyle had not gone to bed as early as eleven in years, and he awoke in the middle of the night. Unable to call back sleep, he climbed out of bed, removed his black pressing rag, and stepped into the front yard. Something made him look up, and he discovered the stars. In Harlem, he could see only the brightest, strongest ones. But now he saw more stars than sequins on a barmaid's dress, and liked them. He sat, then lay down, careful to keep his hands between the wet grass and his hair.

At first he did not hear her thumping toward him. Then her pinched orange-gray face peered down at him, her hair wrapped around tiny spiked metal rollers. "You didn't like your bed?" She wore only a nightgown, drab in the starlight.

He sat up quickly. "I couldn't sleep. Not enough happening." That sounded funny to him and he laughed quietly.

"I know what you mean." She hesitated for a moment, then sat down next to him. The dentist's scheme might work after all. The man might know his wife. Maybe she had some men, but in a very careful way.

Lowering herself down beside him, she gathered up the nightgown to show him knees as square and hard as fist-sized ivory dice. "It's a nice night though."

"Yeah." He had not finished judging her legs.

"They're not much, are they? Maybe that's why . . ." She stopped. "No, that's not why." Then she looked at him. "Mr. Bedlow . . ."

He did not let her finish, pushed her onto her back while his name still bubbled in the air. He did business, like opening a car door, going through the glove compartment, tossing the road maps aside, hoping to find a portable radio or a wallet. She wrapped her thin arms and legs around him, moaned as if in pain.

On hands and knees, he pulled away from her, and discovered she had begun to cry. "Oh, this is bad. This is bad. But . . . I was so hot!" She rolled onto her stomach, muffling sobs in the grass. "This is really bad. I can't do this!"

He patted her shoulder blades, pulled her nightgown over her buttocks, realizing as he tried to comfort her, that the dentist had lied to him. She had waited. Of course, it made no real difference; but he did not want it known that he believed everything people told him.

Finally he got her to stop crying and sit up. But she would not look at him, huddled on the grass, her back to him. "I'm sorry, Mr. Bedlow. I guess you could tell we're having troubles. But I didn't mean to bring you into it."

"Come on, Robena, the sky won't fall down. And call me Carlyle. Mr. Bedlow don't make it now." He moved closer to her, spoke over her shoulder. "What kind of trouble you people got? You own everything, two houses, a big car, and all that. So it can't be money." He believed what he said, but had asked because now he wanted to know the dentist's weaknesses.

She lowered her chin to her chest. "No, it's not money. Yes, it's money." She raised her head and turned toward him. "How old are you?"

He gave himself a few years.

"I'm thirty-six." She waited, let the number die. "Me and my husband, when we went to school, in Washington, it was different, even from your time. We always thought, at least I did—I mean, now I don't know what he really thought—I mean, we thought it was enough for him to be a dentist. You know what I mean?"

All this had little to do with marriage, the kind he knew. He had expected the usual story, the dentist running in the street, chasing after many Mamies before this one. Or perhaps she would think the dentist cheap. He waited.

"But that's not enough anymore. I mean, he's a good dentist. He really is. But they don't care if he's good or not. I always thought they'd care."

Carlyle thought, then realized whom she talked about.

"But they don't. It took me a long time to see that, and after, I didn't want to believe it." She paused. "We got raised to believe we had to be best. My mama always told me, you got to be best in your class."

Carlyle too remembered such words.

"But I was a girl and only supposed to be the best wife I could. So when we got married, I worked so he could go to school full-time. He's a good dentist, but it didn't do any good. When he should've been on the staff of a good clinic, he ended up in Harlem. And when he should've . . ." She shook her head. "This isn't very interesting, is it?"

Carlyle had developed patience in his work; he told her to go on, still hoping she would give him something important.

"The point is when I saw they lied about caring, I looked into everything they said, and you know what? They lied about everything." Her discovery still bewildered her.

"Hell, I known that since I was seven."

She shook her head several times. "No, listen, everything. Even about food. You ever read the small print on a box of ice cream? It's not even ice cream."

"You sound like my little brother." He started to laugh. "He's a Black Jesuit. And you know they crazy."

She ignored him. "What I want is for him to stop working for a year and go around the world. I want to see if what I think is true really is. And I want him to see it. And if it is, maybe we can do just something small. It's not enough for us to sit out here on a little pile of money. I mean, we're supposed to do something good for our race too." She stopped talking then, sat with her chin on her knees, her nightgown bunched around her thighs, leaving Carlyle disappointed.

Then she stood up. "Well, that's my sad tale. Maybe you'll tell me yours one time." She smiled, for the first time.

In the kitchen, she gave him a cup of instant coffee. He read the label, wondering what kind of chemicals the Xs and Ys represented, their action in his stomach. When he had finished the coffee, he returned to his room, retied his head, and climbed into bed.

14

THE DENTIST KNOCKED at his door at nine the next morning, but did not wait for Carlyle to ask him in. "Got through, didn't you. I knew you'd crack it. I hope your man is a good picture-taker. My prints got to come out clear!"

Carlyle propped himself against the bed's headboard. "She may not do it again." He had decided that he would let the dentist believe himself still in charge.

"Everybody knows the first nut is the hardest."

"Maybe so. How you know anyway?"

"I woke up at three and she wasn't in bed. And neither was you. I figured you went someplace together. What'd you think of it?"

"Ain't the best I ever had."

"Me too." The dentist came to the bed's foot. "But with the money you can buy something better." The dentist smiled, good even white teeth, one gold-covered—then closed his lips. "You better drive over to that motel and tell your friend to load his camera."

Carlyle nodded. "What's the plan for today?"

"We got invited to a party. In the late afternoon. We get her drunk; you bring her home, undress her and snap away. I'll make sure you got the house to yourselves." He smiled again. "Me and my Mamie'll make sure, someplace." He laughed, turning to the door. "Get your hook in deep."

"I might throw this one back," M.F.

He opened the door. "Not in my creek, you don't."

But Carlyle did not know that for certain.

As he dressed—in short-sleeved pink silk shirt, white bell-bottoms—he tried to decide exactly what to do. Obviously, he wanted to come out the other end with the dentist's thousand dollars. But then the dentist would have to get his pictures. Carlyle most wanted to get his money, but leave the dentist married to his crazy wife. That would sound good when told at the Grouse. "That dentist thought he had Carlyle, but then Carlyle Bedlow got down to business, do you hear, business!" That meant he had to get the money before the dentist saw the pictures, bad ones. But when he paid the money, the dentist would have to believe the pictures had come out clearly. Carlyle heard himself talking: "She passed out, man. I just sat there beside her in my shorts. We pulled back the covers and Hondo snapped away. They so good we might even sell some." But the pictures would show nothing. He rehearsed his speech while he finished dressing.

He avoided breakfast, wanting the dentist to suffer through a morning with both of his women, imagining that scene as he drove the dentist's car between the trees on his way to visit his friend, the photographer, Hondo Johnson.

"Wait a minute. You say you don't want the pictures to come out?"

"Right."

Hondo sat on the edge of his motel bed in pale-yellow pajamas. "Well, why don't you just give him a blank roll?"

"Because if he ever finds me I can tell him it surprised me too. I can offer to do it again." He looked into Hondo's mirror, checking his hair. "But he won't go for it because no man could do it twice to the same woman. And I'm sorry, doc, but I already spent that money. He ain't got no boys to send after me."

"Come on, man. Why can't we just do it simple? Take the pictures and collect the money." Once Hondo got a plan in his mind, he did not like to change it. He could not improvise. "We'll mess up, man. And I can sure use that money."

"We won't lose the money. We'll take insurance pictures. Good ones, with her legs open and all. I know a man downtown'll buy them." He needed the pictures just in case the dentist did have some boys. "You satisfied now?"

Hondo nodded, did not look happy. His lips poked out under his mustache. "Tell me the signal."

Carlyle had not thought about it. "When I turn out the lights."

Hondo started to laugh. "And how do I shoot pictures in the dark?" Catching Carlyle pleased him.

"You're all right, man." He adjusted his shirt, turned from the mirror. "What about the blinds?"

"That's good. Pull down the blinds. And if they already down, pull them up. Just do something with them blinds." He stood up. "You got that?"

"Right." He liked Hondo. "But I'll try to get her fallen down, so we'll have plenty of time, and she won't know nothing. Then we leave. I never did like no drunken Jones anyway."

15

THE PLAN HAD WORKED. She might even pass out before he got her off the dirt road, into the house and out of her clothes. The party had started at five, and now at ten, still rolled. They had eaten potato salad, fried chicken and greens on paper plates, drinking steadily. The doctors, lawyers, dentists, big-time hustlers got very loud, about baseball, Harlem after the war when they had all begun their careers. Their children, teenagers, gained control of the phonograph, danced hard on the lawn. Carlyle had filled her empty glasses. Finally he asked her if she wanted to go home. Winking at the dentist, he led her out of the house.

In the moonlight, the dirt of the road, half-sand, shone gray. He supported her with a hand on her bony rib-cage. "How you doing?" He did not really want her to answer, and disturb herself.

"I'm doing fine. What did you say?"

"Nothing." They crossed the dentist's grass now, circling a clump of lawn chairs and an umbrella-table, a few steps from the porch. He saw the bushes move and waved at Hondo.

Taking her straight to her bedroom, he turned on the dim table lamp, and began to undress her. She did not resist, lay so limp he did not know if she had stayed awake. He put her clothes onto a chair, returned to the bed and pulled the bed-covers from under her.

"Thanks, baby." The baby sounded strange, meant not for him, but for the dentist.

He undressed to his shorts, went to the window, and pulled down the blinds.

"What's that?" She raised her head, but it weighed too much.

He tried to imitate the dentist. "Nothing, baby."

Hondo banged open the front door, made his way through the living room, bumping into things. He slid the coffee table out of his way. Carlyle went to the bedroom door. "Hey, man, quiet down. Follow my voice."

"Nigger, why didn't you turn on some lights?" He had almost reached the hallway. Carlyle waited at the other end.

"Follow my voice, man."

Now Hondo ran toward him, appeared, in Bermuda shorts and sneakers. Carlyle backed into the room.

Hondo popped into the doorway, stopped. "You expect me to take pictures in this light?" He looked disgusted.

"Quiet down, man." Carlyle whispered. "She ain't out yet."

"I got to have more light. I didn't bring my infrared attachment." He began to focus his camera on the dentist's naked wife.

"Baby?" She rolled to her side, then back. "Who's that?"

"Nobody. Close your eyes. I'm turning on the top light."

She did not answer. He waited, then switched it on. For a few seconds, he could not see Hondo. "All right?"

"I think so." He put the camera to his face again. "But I can't be sure until I read the meter."

"Come on, Hondo. We ain't got time for that." She would wake up. Somehow he knew it.

"Always got time. What if we don't get our insurance pictures?" He took a light-meter from his pocket, advanced on her, held it over her navel.

Carlyle sat down on the bed. "How you doing, baby?" He patted her shoulder.

Her eyes stayed closed. "Who's that just now?"

"A man." He leaned over, kissed her cheek.

"I got it now, Carlyle." Hondo moved to the foot of the bed. "One point four. But I got to do it in seconds so you can't move."

"Who's that voice?" She raised herself to her elbows, looked up into Hondo's lens. "Who's he?"

"Now hold it."

But she had already moved, scrambling to the edge of the bed. "He got you to do this!"

Carlyle reached out for her, but she broke away, and jumped for the closet. "He'll never get it now!" She pulled the door behind her.

Carlyle did not follow her. He could easily open the closet door, but that would do no good. She had to be in bed, with a man, looking either surprised or happy, but not struggling. "You better come out of there, Robena." He put a threat into his voice, but did not mean it. She had to imprison herself while he thought. He knew what he had to do: to convince her to pose for the pictures.

He looked at Hondo, still busy with final adjustments, then stood up. "Listen, you can't stay in there all night. Nobody's coming to rescue you." He put his mouth close to the door.

"And nobody's getting a divorce neither." She started to scold him. "I thought you was nice."

"I am. Come on out."

Hondo sat on the bed, camera waiting.

"You're not nice." She paused, cleared her nose. "You make love to women for money." She sniffled again.

"Me? Listen, I came out here with Mamie. Your husband's nurse?"

"I know her. She got a crush on him."

"No, she don't." He waited; she did not speak. "She's with me, but then last night you and me got into something special. And your husband found out, and said he'd make a lot of trouble for me if I didn't get his pictures. He got me in a terrible spot."

She paused for a moment. "First of all, you didn't even talk to Mamie, all the way out in the car. And second, where did you get a cameraman so fast?"

The dentist had married a smart woman. "You acting real stupid. What you want with a man who don't want you?"

"He does so want me." She did not believe herself.

"No, he don't. He wants Mamie. He wants to marry her." His voice grew cold, the way he talked to policemen as long as their guns remained buried under blue winter coats. "And he's paying me lots of money to get him a divorce."

She waited again, crying behind the closet door. "Well, he's not getting it."

"Listen, Robena." He bent closer, softened his tone. "Face it, baby. He don't want you. He don't want anything about you. He don't want to go around the world with you. He thinks you're crazy. Give the man his pictures."

And she did.

16

Hondo took the clearest pictures any magistrate would ever accept into evidence. The woman sat on the bed, bare to the waist. She looked sad, her infidelity uncovered. The young hoodlum beside her, his hair shiny and slightly waved, did not at all resemble her dentist husband.

Carlyle decided against trying for extra money. One thousand would do him a while. The dentist paid him, in cash, the following Monday evening.

He had long since turned the money into a belted camel's-hair overcoat, shoes, some perfume for his children's mothers, when next he heard from the dentist's wife. She had mailed a postcard to him care of the Grouse. It came from Europe:

> *Hello. We here on our honeymoon.*
> *My husband is a dentist from*
> *(the ink had smeared) in Africa.*
> *Best wishes, Robena (remember?)*

At first he could not remember. Her handwriting did not make a face. Robena sounded like somebody pretty jacked up. That brown girl from Atlanta joining her brother in Germany? A stewardess? That teenager in the blue dress and pink barrettes who wandered into the Grouse saying she had lost her way to Westchester? Where in the city had he met a Robena? The Bronx? Brooklyn? The Village? The Westside? Harlem?

He remembered the hen; it have surprise him, n he thinked about it for aWhile in the Overhaul, we may rate him n Mr. Charcoyle too right off centered and beginning tinfur subsistory infemination about his Malma from dottold, long-furgoted pegTail.

Dust, we may away ouSelfs from the Langleash language fo aPerusol o'some Sauce-matourial gleanerd from dPages o'dDialy Citysun, n aCause, in dTongue o'Now Afreequerquenne, seeng z'Mr. Chacallo vbegin tclose dGap in dOwnderstanding o'dFront o'hExpierience n tspy dRelayshinship betwin hId-self n dhat:

Dappy duoWifed Mr. 521th Street Dentoost, tendng Home on dTanagent, makeng dRound o'Harem-nicepots wi spicey Piece-girl, Rojena Shadrack. DBoys at B.B.s Bubbershop recommand he branch dhat Hypocritimus on aTree n call dhem by dhei'riteful Name;

Polley Gomez (note ed. chimer-about-tone), inrolld by h'well-pressd Prisonoir-parents in d'exclusively cashionable OuLadle o'dGriddle School, where dSupperintender o'Spoart, Chaf Childmascher, racently varrive from Upcellar's Jan Freize Skol wi Orders tenrumpture dPreseedngs in dLockeroom. HAim: tdimfuse dDeezs n dDoozs, wi special Infantsis on dGuiles. He vfill Poll fool o'Nounsense, n dhen vsend her down hWay twarble hWhim tWham, at lease twenty itch Foughtnight, n vlove ditto, who sayd: "He do'nt'have aChance? He

Polley Gomez

conduit. V-dGirls have mo'in dheiBuddys, baby? Who Star Tit wi More?"

Tommy Tambo, n hBalkick-boygirl Bwide, Fredarichard, bleching in dWeeds wi dhat lillBoarboy no mater what Toymay Taymbow doy aboutit, who vreceive aVicette from Anspectre Theopolice Heeley, who vhad him aHymn o 77 (runreddrunn!)

Tommy Tambo and Fredarichard

followng dUnveilng o'hApoxalipical-Hymenall. (Coyez, Clyle, ne pas plier, but if you creases it, dHats all on tyou.) Later Frigericha vcall dInspectar at dSquid Room, where she vslum, tlet him know hHubboy, Tubby, vgiver Trouble. She sayd hHead she vshed, hizid she seed, n cdntgig it. D'fakeCat vtow over dhere, n nopd Tim's Noirbet, giveng d'well-tressd Entercontainer dAdmoanition: "We know you myride to her, but don't startreating that Murphy like a yam!"

Said Alfalah, oilrich Ptomentake from dMiddleleast, sharkng Aimbossy Row by proposeng dhat dGovermint trade hGypverment ouWoemans fo Earlmeralds n Industraildiemands. He explaned at Corkineary Air, portng aPip, n emppland hSelf dhis aWhy: "We knead dWomn, n you nab d'hostilepal Beds."

Hexilency Joke Barney Popachill, dRector o'dTheor Yeth Odinization's Free Launch Progrom n what he vanswored when he closed hittite: "I am not in the babit to be asterix my reputation for tough Moutheadness by being fussed tan, sir, the questions of beachboys, if he knows what's god for him. After all, I roed himher over, flour free."

Vitchis Moroless Krecht, in hWay famous Suregun from Bactavaria, who vmake Headslines aFew Vix ago by fleeng dFreyr-world fo dFryworld n dCharms o'aCuti calld Hot-Fingers Dancerabar, in dCotton's Paw: "I waltz dieng, so I gulf for vie, not?"

Jigglebody Jackson, n what she vsay after dhatMan wi dGun vbrak in hDressng-roamng around in n over hDraws, dhen falld on hKnees n begd n plegd wi her tgive him a'silver Dunceng-shoe wi dSpikeheel n coalSole: "But, butteie, dhen I lllimp too."

DALDERMAN CELEBRATE HCINQUACENTURY
LYMBNG BUT LIMBERSTILL

Flashy former Falldman, C. C. "Af" Wrhygin sitng

Vitchis Moroless Krecht and HotFingers Dancerabar

in aRocker celebrightng hHundreadth-berthday, stroked a'cateyed firmer Seamtress, Maeba, h'twenty-two-yeahold Waif, n vreflect on h'forty omo times twelve Years in d'lococal Polittlecarl-scene: "We vhave ouUpsandownes, ouBrackn-forths, ouOverenders, n I douane dhey always pious by. African

Jigglebody Jackson

Alley vntget remoteld yet. When it lllook butter, Ursa llshow us aPair o'Steal-pants."

DJettyson visk d'begrizzled Bestaboredon tcommint dCoinage o'h'adequated Parlens t'dEvents o'd'changeng Toaday:

"I vsee dSameting z'dissolver d'lost few Yeas. I vmake dRide tNewhoundland. I vsofa dSeesickness too. But I vmake mSelf aTrade wi Smith n Black, Anvils, tpay mPassout Money. I vemployer mSellf. Any Ting vdo it if he could it around in dMouth in hHead. Dawn, sir, by yOreself n aMaMa n, ibung her, ije ySelfs. Muvaut! Splitez!"

DCityson vset back. "Al, man, sitinbull again."

"Now you take dEngines, powr Rusticks. Dhey vwin dBabyll, but dhey lllose dWar dSpite dheiSoot fo it. Soon z'we get ouBubbettes away from dheiWigworm, n out dBuckseat. Taker care tsetter up! Buy hBack wi Cloth tdrape. Better tsweeten it. She lltaste less bitter. Salt needd here! No leaker allowd! It silk at dPourtea, n hell on dBroadway goeng Home. Besides when Mimmae bwabeng she get boohoozy about hDefilment, hSin (so-cold), wi'out realizeng Sirvilefall vmake it necesairey. Sew do'ntunravel dhat Yawn about hStrayness. Mostly we vencountourd superior Fearpower, n Milema vsunse a'hard Wonter awintng. Dhen, we vrun ouGamebit under aCloud o'Moonbombs, aBag o'Ballwire, aWoe o'Warmbate away from Momoa's Minny mansons. We vntsee aDrop in aWater's Chance o'Saylng high n out o'dHat-Place. But nummo, bubbah! We vestablish aContitact! He he ee e e e e s s h she up! Lissend:"

Doom dicker doom, doomdoom, doom ticker doom doom tickerdoom. Dumber ticker ticker doom, dicker bum, ticker ticker dumb, ticker bum, doom boom.

What he say, Jim? Crow me not.

Dhat dHaulting dhat dHeyman vdefyne z'human in us, dhat dTrulyafriman, not what Mr. Chill vname dHueman, which, I duboilieave, dDrim o'dHair o'dEnertgee o'dMomery o'dSpearit o'd'orbiginal whammer-warshipng, akernitng onmanic Trolegodiet! I know what I vnez! I row at hat I wor! It vhide in mId n mEd n dpAlm o'mAnd. MFeet dhat I vsir-survive data n all.

But it haves! N dBook I vfind in aStorehrum o'd'recently-opend Kingstomb outside New Afriquequergy—DVOYAGOS O'PRINCE WOLE—dhat telve int'dRelationship betwine we-Selfs n d'cold Glareys o'Stunangle, aManumental Campas North o'dChiliwatube Reder, prove mPrint.

DhisBook talk about dHidstorycal-fact dhat dNoirmans vexplore Sections o'dNorman's Whorl (befo dheiErrora vrobd dFlabric o'Trainkillity) in dhei'neo-glitteryst Slips o'dDay. Can-you llhear what we vsay when we vsaw it?

Look ata dhem paintd-white Rocks!

Why, isdhey lacepay nentey veney inishdfey? N aftydrey? N oldkay?

Ookley at dOundgray n dChilltrees!

Mans, d'wholeTing aPretrock's Knightmare. Let summon else build it up. Stop Construction on dCompass! Tow dBowts! Pack dhem Oats! Plank dhat Oak! Knock dhaDock, dhat docker doom dicker dock, tick tick, doom ticker dock, doom ticker dark, ticker ticker dark, doomdoom, dicker doom.

Tonde, you get dPepper?

Listen, baby, Prince Wolle vsay heed him n out!

Ebonybody abode? Seventeneightan, ninetaileantwenty. Mr. Charchile, where be yGlowarm?

You vntsin her easer? Stop in dName o'Loaf! We vlift hBe-hind! Boatsun, can Woell turn back?

No cain do, bubh. DMeteo just vreport Gladestone Glaciar n all dGlimstems moveng int'dSlot. Steak cool; she llget some boof tbuy hSunhouse other.

What vhaptring tyou, Mr. Choco, leaveng yGloray tget hWay layd? Why you do'nt yet readyize you llntgrow aFernily widoubt aSun n dOrder o two? You canntbreak yEggs like Dhat, man. You dumpty ySelf when you nthumptyng yon energinger-bread Lady.

Vnt-Anybuddys tell you dWord against Muffiocrity n Sick-cand Closs Tickets at dWhale's Closet? Do'nt-you know dFinger trise tget out o'dhisEmenar? No? Dhat dIt n day dicker doom! Lyrn dLesson! You may concider ySoulf fly z'aFreyr widowter, but d'actyall Tally run a'huntrod Vicions off aTassel on aFlag chaind t'aBoat.

Flashy former Falldman, C. C. "Af" Wrhygin, and Maeba h'twenty-two-yeahold Waif

17

In the mist on the dock an the harbour bay the river around the ighland below the graytestity of the whale Titinac Hold, programing with its very stropheness the pore of Her Stainted Magester, Friginia, her floorashing tredding abyssness in the slunken, soiltry, saveage, stuductive ports of the call, whipped gully its tussels, as if she, three chairs on the old gill, siggnalled the larrival upover decks laudly of Lord Limph, Childe d'Lacquedouster, an Amissery Emorable in the Aimpyre's Nervy.

The men asymboled to ear rim constitchuted as sourly an aggressionation of howdy, taphammerfisted, fablefuddled feemen as, keenly, had seen the lee of Siamapurr. Present and prim stood Master Hench, First G'd.Rt.A'm, straight-sucked, stake-sudsed, the only burn seamoan amoon them, a saint asea, but inland an insand stabber of lassoes, scarving up inyards before biling bones in bullyearn (slightly seasoned, sinner until croaked).

The casual orbserver might desire to turnderway from both

boht and crew at the site of Hitch; but conning his ed, he vood encounter Herr Ehrr, derr Forst Stiward, whein aloofen an oven stouffer, graiduate in veaporncocking from Grufhousand, one of his two owls putsch-covered. Not tore forget us Gunner Hawnson, not so dippily involved save in Dollarware; or Peat Hyveston, a wooden shoe for a leg—though man to min, measuring measle to pipple, Lurd Lampalot's limes had dumped from Lumdum's lums, by the grave of gunvicted, thence, grumbled off to serve a worm in Her Voyagin Magi'sty's chips. It iwaz on of these—T.Y.S. Woten's Wessel—which Lanece Limp comeondeared.

The herd hord stump-feets from bhelow, and Hack, whip wiping wildely and woundwashed, swabbed the many acidely, making quai for Lide Lumanury's uhrival.

Oever, the opening doris had revealed the sprightly brittle Benyangian boatboy, Bo Changles, a kwute waddle fellow with a ponepensity to expand within his kneebreetches and wastecoat, though when Load Loom speared him in a tokenboat through the pocket mirror one afternoird off the cusp of Ymom-samaman, he looked depositively all thin.

Teeny, a baby he in fact washed, (not at all to make a Mose a Morses, though to repose the poseabilities of dustituation, he could bring them the beat in a certain water down the ways, jes us like Sangmonde Froid cooled the Allemammer team, 4-1 minute's time, though kneed alltimetely by Audolf and his tiwas yochtling odors) and bathed him in snow hite, lining the cellar plyroom with pictures of him being good, beng bagd but in all ways keeping him emported in the footlockers at the ankle of his brain.

Lynmp hoped, as he remarked it ti Rudderwick of Venice, Whaler like himself, that, as his aid, regarding less of his slumming list of wit, and of certain fociel complexionities—his nose of run, his lip of skin, his overall greasy, Hugh-dear—the little pickapeppa would turn an Enguishman yet, as gode as many of your Tigs, Dains or Harald Fenrirs.

But Hak had ever stoked a stomp on Chaggle's bow. "Spades, Beamish, if we went wind-up without warrant."

"Don't worry, Mr. Phox. He'll come up in a micnute," Choke ashored deminimem.

Hick steifled his aarrm, prepared to rook Chick's nog. "Be thee without mannerisms of pealty? Where's yee servience when you dress Master Hex?"

Chaca chivaled. "Come on, my sir, be you, man."

"Humunhuh?"

"Hoosee! What are you doe-wing with this weet title laddie?" Fore indood, Laimpule had skippled upon deck, his cuttles slient, his heels hispy. "Don't you know this is my personel savant? Come a her, sun."

Chag mated his ground, resigning about time, shoking the head's world.

"Coma to me, Chookie. I've bought a surprise for you. Calm on out, Wedely-dear."

The hubburb doors slidely soapened to a russelle of sulk powdering a poute, a furdrove fuller bushes, a pinpint of ladderpadder cheetihose, sverevel knocky neezen, two fletschy shudderblades, one large wopfer in the middle, a petipilvis off to one side and no whitter than a pain of window, glassblyeyes calling to mine the chillchurls of the House of Assguard. "Heelo, Chit."

But that whooshn't his windy near as he could reember her, though he knew its suckled meaning.

"Ates this? A wruinman abroad?" Hache, taking two fresh chups from the norest swale, pounded Limp's boff, handsiftedly. "Rag nor rocker headed if he torches haarr!"

Thanks, but I don't want cheese in fish.

"Lamplear, tele Hunch to shut up." She beered her teesks. "I wamp the chigger, Daddy, eight inch to bar. Wheely."

Miss Chill? Pardon me, but—

Whapt snacked Haunch's scatterninetails. "I bliv yiv bid tiribly inviting this Ifrikin tithy pirty."

Maybe I be excused, please?

"I want you. Holy." Talonese fingersnails pierced his ear, hire breathsts in his face. "Golly me, Wole."

No.

"I want you, Wally."

"Sure, Lynn. But not now. I mean, I think he's up there."

"Well?" They whispered.

"Well?"

Chig looked at his watch, read the glow-dial's twelve o'clock, but did not know whether that meant midnight or noon. Third-class cabins had no windows.

"What do you want to do?"

"I want you, Wally. Now."

"With him up there? He might wake up."

"Oh, Wally."

Chig wondered why his dream's Wendy had blond hair. Wendy's hair had hung long and black. On their first date, three days after the Assassination, he had longed to lose his fingers in it. But they had only talked.

"I'm really upset with you, Wally."

"But we can't just, you know . . . Golly. With him up there? We can wait until he goes out."

"When does he go out?"

"I don't know. When he wakes up."

On their second date, she had invited him to her apartment, one big room and a kitchen in the Old City. Timidly, he had taken her hand and they had passed the fallen pillars of a Roman temple, into her courtyard, three neighborwomen watching them. Wendy had filled her room with exotic things: African material nailed to the white walls, paintings, two pieces of African sculpture. She owned a phonograph, plenty of records. Uncomfortable in her rooms, he had spilled his coffee.

"Why don't you wake him up and ask him to leave?"

"I hardly know him, Lynn. Besides, you're not even supposed to be here."

"That's nice, Wally. And you even know what Mr. Oglethrope said."

Chig had awakened on his stomach, now rolled to his side. He hoped they would hear him, panic, and make themselves respectable.

"Lynn? He's waking up."

"Shhh."

After their third date, a movie full of swords, sails, ships and sea, they had made love. Expecting only to serve coffee and some hard native cake, he had asked her to his room. Just inside the door, she had turned, her eyes closed; he had never put on the coffee pot. She told him she liked him better than any man she had met since leaving Virginia.

"He only turned over. Oh, Wally, I want you so bad." She kissed him, a series of little lip-clicks.

Wendy had kissed him just once, in the doorway. Afterwards, he had walked her home, afraid to ask her to stay. At her door, she extended her hand. The next day, he called her. She did not answer. The day after that, he took her some flowers. Her landlady, an old face in a turret window, told him that *modeurnala* Whitman had departed.

"Hey!" Wally jumped, rocking Chig's bunk. "What're you doing?"

She answered, a moan, muffled.

"Come on, Lynn." He took a breath. "Don't do that."

Chig rolled to his back, to his other side, to his back again.

They quieted. Perhaps he should speak and let them share his embarrassment. But he did not want to embarrass them. He shifted again, hoping they would catch his hint.

"He's really waking up." Wally's voice went higher.

"But it's all right now." Her voice had deepened. "We can be quiet."

"Come on, Lynn. Let's go for a swim." He paused. "Maybe we're missing lunch."

"You see? He stopped moving. We can be real quiet. You see? Come on, Wally. Really. Really. Wally. Oh, Wally."

Wally began to hum, one tone, way high up. Chig rolled again, but they did not hear him.

"Oh, Wally. Oh, Wally. Oh, golly me, Wally. Golly me. Golly me. Oh. Golly me. Wally. Wally? Oh, Wally. Really? Oh, Wally!" He had stopped humming. "Oh, Wally." She sighed. "Wally, why'd you do that?"

"I just couldn't help it."

He listened to them adjust their clothes, their combs crackling the electricity in their hair.

"Are you all right, Lynn?"

"I want a raspberry soda. You think I can have that?"

When they had gone, Chig climbed down from his bunk and washed his face. After Wendy disappeared, he had left the city. For the next ten months, he had travelled to all the capitals of Europe, a month here, two there, then decided he had stayed in Europe too long. The time had arrived to return to the United States.

He had missed lunch, but most of the ship's passengers remained over coffee in the dining room. The decks shone bare. He leaned on the railing and watched the scar of water leading to the horizon, to Europe. The United States waited behind him, a day away, getting closer all the time.

"Get locked out, Mr. Dunford?"

Chig fought a smile, then let it come. "Yes. How you feeling today, Wally?"

"Great." He nodded; the hard wind blew a little hole in the back of his head. "I made a lot of noise this morning. I hope I didn't wake you up." He tried to look at Chig, could not.

"I sleep like a stone, Wally."

"Great." He stared at Chig, secure now. His eyes glittered light-brown, almost golden, the eyes of a boy who had delivered newspapers from a bike and never missed a porch. "Great."

"Well . . ." Chig sighed; he wanted Wally to leave.

But Wally's attention had wandered upward, and now, mouth open, his lips O-ed, he gazed at something just above Chig's head. "She must be a movie star, huh, Mr. Dunford?"

"Who?"

"Her up there. She's really something."

On the first-class deck, the girl's orange shorts and long, tanned legs gleamed. A narrow orange ribbon pulled her black hair back from her face. Chig looked, looked again, at Wendy. Wow.

Woooee! He was alone on the deck, looking up at the empty captain's pilothouse. The steering wheel was whirling back and forth. He was turning away from the pilothouse. He was walking toward the swimming pool. It was empty, frozen solid. Nobody was skating. He was walking along the deck. His hand was touching the smooth steel railing. It was cold. He was not wearing his overcoat. He was cold. He was wondering where everybody was.

He was thinking that everybody was inside. He was going into the snack bar. It was cold as a meat locker. The juice in the globe in the snack bar was frozen, green and stiff like the swimming pool was.

He was paying his fare. He was leaving a quarter on the bar. The profile of President Lockie was on the quarter. He was walking out of the snack bar. He was walking to the railing. He was looking at an island. The boat was passing the island. The boat was going out to sea.

He was deciding to jump off the boat. He was removing his shoes. He was pulling off his socks. He was rolling up his cuffs. He was climbing the cold railing. He was jumping into the water.

He was swimming. It was cold. He was swimming. It was cold. He was swimming. He was cold. He was swimming. He was gaining on the shore.

The shore was a rocky beach. Behind the beach was a forest of little pine trees and little oak trees. His right foot was touching the cold rocks in the cold water. He was wading out of the cold water. He was standing on the rocky beach. He was hearing drums. He was tiptoeing toward the forest. The forest was a room of forest. The forest top was only as high as an old kitchen's ceiling. He was hungry. He was looking around the forest for some food. He was looking at a man.

"Now on, Y. M. just not gone to have a bite of it!"

The man's head was platted. The hair was pulled away tight from the cowpaths. The skin in the cowpaths was shining in the cold sunlight.

"Not eden for a might! Disghastling!" The man was sucking his tongue. "Why riff I have a known wee wood get such acomeadateons, Eva never come. Imatchin! I thought at least we wood have a smimmyhole. And the way they tearing my beardzies zappoline! A baiterful guile. The younger brothers juster lover. We designed some exquivite sacklesses for us to ware our shows. Pumps too. Ebon the barbellboy binked. But assoon as we tootled into ouDressingroom to groom, the house dicked bourged in and priced her under a rest. I wask reaming, nor nau naw, but he deadened stop.

"Supertime, suppletime," he ketpots aying.

"Well, you know out dare? on the grittlefield? where they roost gwineys and foul around, where they billed the barnfire for the singe out? That's where the pot ides. A pigpot, with a pigfur yunder it, and every Pogmy had a pork and a poon, and annapolkins under day chins. And my prototypist, Gluma, stewed boiling in that great pig kettle of potion with potato, pudding and toynips, stoong! All that invitement wafting and not a bee yet to buzz for it."

Who you wrapping a boat?

"My bead who bring the bracers. You mysht noah. Glimmermaid Johnsin? We straveling togather wherever we meight."

In a kattle?

The man was nodding. "And them Packmies dancing, and dhem pillagemies pulping, and doom pickles puffing. Wutheringing of drums too. Poo poo: pom pom: boomboom: boombam: bambim: bimbim: bingbing, and like, Chorloyal, I seen that kind of rhyvenom bamsness before. Bumbum bombom be saying gogo, Boatorfly, or gooses'll cook roast ribs rooster ripped, ripetty, a pity a piety a pything, a porgmytom, a porkmeatom, a parkmetom, a arkpetom, a automotom, a intommybedmatom, a tatmytummytom, the tunnel tomtom telling Butt tomes too moany of them, a tomsorrow of them and nusa lost, lost, lost. Whooa! I was so lost. But how could die live without that absolutely beautiful boy?"

Carlyle wore sunglasses tinted dark gray. They filtered the glare, made the streets seem darker even than night. He had slept behind them. "You asking me, Butterfly?"

"Of course, baby." Butterfly took his eyes from the Avenue for an instant, flashed them Carlyle's way. "But I don't expect an answer." He tossed his shoulders, smiled.

Carlyle lifted his head from the back of the seat. "You a good driver, Butterfly. I thought I was home in bed."

"I know you comfortable, baby." He blew Carlyle a kiss. "But you must let me finish telling my story. He was just beautiful, and we'd go away weekends upstate to Wee Wood Hotel. It was wonderful."

They had come to within a block of the Grouse. "You better hurry, Butterfly."

"You terrible to me, Carlyle." But he smiled.

"How it come out, Butterfly?"

"I was very unhappy for about two months." He double-parked beside the corner car, turned to Carlyle. "But I'm not unhappy anymore."

Carlyle opened the door, put his feet outside. "Anybody I know?" He felt the cold wind on his ankles, stood up.

"You know him very well."

He leaned into the car. "Thanks for the ride, Butterfly."

"Good night, baby."

Carlyle closed the door, waved at Butterfly through the glass, watched the lemon-yellow boat-wide automobile glide into traffic.

Standing in the cold air, he realized he wanted some barbecue and macaroni salad. He started walking toward the Silver Dinner Diner, sandwiched between two apartment buildings a few doors from the Grouse.

Glora worked without her wig. Her natural hair made a large round headdress. "You seen Cooley, Carlyle?"

"Not tonight." He sat down on a counter stool, smiled at her, hoping she would give back her special smile, but Cooley owned her mind. "Give me some ribs, Glora."

"You want to sit here, or with your friend?"

"What friend?"

She pointed into the back. Hondo sat in the farthest back booth, his head hanging over a hamburger steak, an untouched pile of rice and peas.

"He ain't a friend; he's a brother." He got up. "You a sister or a friend?"

"What you say, brother?"

They both laughed. But she stopped quickly. Her full, soft mouth took a gold tooth well.

"Put some macaroni salad with them ribs." He walked into the diner's shadows, slid in across from Hondo and waited for his friend to look up. Hondo continued to stare at his plate.

Carlyle shook his arm. "How you doing, man?"

"I look like I got my health, don't I?" He blinked at Carlyle. "I look like I'm healthy, right? Or am I wrong?"

"You're right."

"Well, I'm dying this Thursday." He spoke as if he expected Carlyle to doubt him.

"Why you pick Thursday?"

"It got picked for me. Ride that a minute."

Carlyle had begun to admire Hondo's plate, now raised his hand, turned and told Glora to change his macaroni salad to rice and peas. "And punch E.7 three times."

"Three times?" From the street end of the diner, Glora smiled. "One time, then I'll make my selections."

Carlyle shrugged. "Why Thursday?"

"Because who knows why that devil picks Thursday? He just say Thursday."

"Who?"

Hondo had waited for him to ask. "The Devil, man." He paused, announced. "I have sold my soul to the Devil."

Carlyle nodded. "And Thursday he collecting?"

"That's what he told me."

"How much you get for it?"

Hondo had not expected that question, lowered his head. "Well, I didn't exactly get no cash money. I made more like a trade."

"A trade? You mean you gave your soul to the Devil and didn't get no money?" For once, Hondo had stayed ahead of him. Carlyle still did not know what game Hondo played. "What did you get?"

"My mama's health."

"Your mama's health? When your mama get sick? You didn't have to sell your soul, man. I could've let you hold some money." He offered Hondo a handle if he needed one.

But Hondo did not seem to want money now. "This happened a little time back, and not to say you ain't doing good, but I didn't believe you could let me have the money I needed for my mama's operation. I needed more zeros than a zoo need zebras! I said, what? Doc, you must be crazy. When he told me the price. But I was crazy. Money. I needed money's mama, bubbah." He shook his head. "Man, I tried skleventy-eleven ways to get that money, couldn't raise a damn dime. Until I seen this ad in The Citizen: WE LOAN TO ANYBODY, with a office right in the neighborhood, way over in the east one-thirties. So I walk over, bust in, and tell the man about my mama. Nice, nice, little fat Latin-like cat sat me in a chair in his two-room office suite, just him and a blonde of a secretary jumping around."

Glora arrived with his plate. Hondo waited until he had Carlyle's attention before he continued.

"I understand your problem, Mr. Johnson, he say. And then he says to me real calm, Carlyle, I'm the Devil, but he wasn't handsome enough and he was too short. I didn't believe him. But he deals his deal. My soul for my mama's health. I got mad. You mean you ain't even giving me some bitches on the side, and a car with a tank full of gas? He shaking his head. Souls's cheap as chickens nowadays, Mr. Johnson. And he knows because I told him I can't get the money from no place else. So I signed up, and tonight he told me this Thursday my bird gets plucked."

19

He felt feathery-light, wondered if he still slept, then decided he did not care. Dream or not, she stood there—and he began to wave his arms and shout her name. He loved saying it: Wendy, again. "Wendy!"

Wally followed, suggesting that Chig ask for her autograph.

"Why, hello, Chig." She looked down at him, raised her hand. She had tanned more deeply than he remembered her; perhaps she had spent the ten months on the Spanish islands. If he had concentrated on Spain, he might have found her. But he had found her anyway.

"How've you been?" He cupped his mouth, shouted up at her. The sun on her orange shorts made him squint.

"Go on ask her, Mr. Dunford. I bet she'll give you one."

Wendy had spoken at the same time; he had not heard her answer. Except for the orange ribbon, she had not tied her hair. "What did you say?"

"I said I'm fine. And would you buy me a drink?" She nodded, directing his answer.

He began to nod his head. "All right. Where can we meet?"

To speak to her taxed his mind; looking almost overcame him: she leaned over the railing, her hair glistening, her face an oval sun, warming him in its dark glow, her eyes wide-set, set deep and dark-brown, her nose broad at the bridge, a trifle hooked, her mouth, her lips full, talking now: "Did you hear me? I'll come down there, to the third-class lounge."

"All right. All right." He raised his wrist, tapped his watch. "What time?"

"Four o'clock?"

"Good." He wondered what he would do for the next three hours, waiting.

"See you then." She wiggled her fingers, stepped back from the railing.

"See you, Wendy."

"She didn't hear you." Wally owned buck-teeth, two little ivory doors set in his face of freckled skin. Two days before, he had told Chig that in his town some kids called him Red. "Did you hear me, Mr. Dunford? She didn't hear you."

Chig smiled. "I know."

"You met her before, Mr. Dunford?"

He shook his head. "I'm not sure, Wally."

"Huh?" His mouth opened slightly. "Hey, you want a drink? Alcohol's real cheap on this boat. Me and my girl got really crashed last night."

Chig picked his comment carefully. "I didn't know you had a girl, Wally."

"Sure. We're on the same TYO Tour. We went to the same school, but I didn't meet her until we both happened to be at TYO's Upstate Fun-For-All in Gully City."

Chig felt confused. "I didn't know you were on a tour." He would have to arrange anew his impressions of Wally. "How many are you?"

"Seventy, counting Mr. Oglethrope."

"Seventy? I thought you were travelling alone, Wally."

"With my Dad? He got real mad when I even first asked him about going to Europe. With TYO. Even though he's in it." Wally paused, opened his eyes with a smile. "Hey, would you like to meet my girl? Just as long as Mr. Oglethrope doesn't catch us."

Chig wondered whether Wally wanted to tell him something, confess, seek advice or comfort. "Doing what?"

"Huh?" The question surprised Wally, made him shrug. "Well, you know about TYO, don't you, Mr. Dunford?"

"Nothing." Chig guessed. "But they don't want you to drink?"

Wally's eyes blinked. "Ya, ya no drinking." He hurried back to his idea. "But what I want is for my girl to meet you." He took Chig's elbow, pulled him across the deck. "Come on, Mr. Dunford."

Chig wanted to prepare himself for his date with Wendy, but he allowed Wally to lead him toward the door of the third-class lounge.

"She's mad at me," Wally explained. "We had a little spat. And we really shouldn't be talking, but it's real important she gets to meet you."

"Why me, Wally?"

They stepped over a high doorsill into the lounge.

"Because when we get married, she wants to move East, and I just want her to meet the kind of people she'll meet there."

Chig smiled, but Wally did not see. "What kind of people, specifically?"

"Huh?" Wally's face seemed all round holes, mouth, nostrils, eyes, freckles. "Negro People." His voice stayed flat. "I heard the East is full of them, just like you." His gaze drifted.

Chig followed the line of his eyes to the face of a teen-aged girl, reading, now lowering her magazine to her lap, revealing her starched white blouse printed in tiny yellow flowers. She had pulled short, straight chestnut-colored hair back from her face with two large pale-red barrettes. "Hi, Wally."

"Hi, Lynn. You reading?"

"Ya. But I was almost finished."

"Lynn? I want you to meet the man I live with. Mr. Dunford."

Her head swiveled slowly, two silver-blue pupils turning his way. "I didn't see you." Her eyelashes grew thin, her eyebrows smudges on her milky skin. "Hi. I'm Lynn."

"Hello, Lynn." He waited in vain for her to extend her hand.

"Wally and me had a fight."

"Yes." He wondered why she told him. "Nothing serious, I hope."

"Sit down, Mr. Dunford, and I'll get some drinks. You want one, Lynn?"

Chig sat in a large chair welded to the boat, one of four such chairs around a low round table.

Lynn looked up at the standing Wally. "Liquor, you mean?" She made a face; her silver eyes blinked once. "Are you having one?"

"A little drink never hurt anybody." Wally put his hand into a pocket of his chino pants, rattled his keys. "That's what my Dad says."

"But Dad Burison doesn't let you drink, Wally."

"Hell!" Wally dropped into his chair.

"But you can have a drink if you want, Wally. I didn't say you couldn't." She put her magazine on the table. Chig wanted to pick it up, leaf through it, but knew that would seem rude.

"See, Mr. Dunford?" Wally appealed to him. "She's just like my Mom. She didn't want me to go to Europe either. But Lynn talked her into it."

"You said you were real glad Mom Burison liked me, Wally.

And you wanted to go with TYO too. We both said we'd learn a lot."

"Wally's probably a little nervous about your fight, Lynn." Chig did not want to witness an argument. "And he wanted me to meet you." She did not react. "He did, Lynn."

"I don't know why if he feels that way, Mr. Dunford."

"What way, Lynn? What way? I didn't even say anything."

"You made me out somebody's mother who ruled them like a queen from the sky." Her chin began to wibble.

"Well, why didn't you let me have one little drink?"

"I turned up my nose because I didn't want one, Wally." Her chin stopped. "You know Mr. Oglethrope said TYO Tour Juniors weren't to be allowed to drink."

Wally sat up in his chair. "But he made a lot of other rules too, that you break."

"You should be real glad—"

"Did you notice, Wally? Everybody's gone."

"Huh, Mr. Dunford?"

Except for the bar steward, mooning at a porthole, the lounge had emptied. A game of cards lay incompleted on a nearby table. The old ladies, going to summer with sons they had not seen in decades, had left the big chairs they claimed each morning.

"I'll ask." He stood up, wanting time to spend alone, to think of Wendy. "I'll be right back."

The bar steward spoke English well enough to let Chig understand that everybody had gone to his lifeboat. "To go there if you will have to go there, sir."

Chig returned to Lynn and Wally. "He says there's a lifeboat drill."

"It's one-forty already?" Lynn took a pocket watch from her gray denim Bermuda shorts. "Mr. Oglethrope'll be really mad at me. We're in the same position, the second-class ballroom."

"Do we go there too, Lynn?"

She stood up, making a fist around her watch. "No, Wally, it goes by room. Mr. Oglethrope sleeps across the hall from me." She walked away on pink lowcut sneakers.

Reasoning that the back of their door might bear the information, Chig and Wally returned to the cabin. They had guessed correctly. The assembly area was the third-class infirmary, which, if Wally remembered rightly, was two decks down. "I'm almost sure it is."

They left the cabin, and taking the nearest staircase, came out into a passageway a little too narrow and shabby for use by any but the ship's crew. This passageway ended in two more, one going to the right, the other to the left. Under his feet, Chig felt the engine breaking itself over and over. "Let's forget it, Wally. We're lost."

"No, really, Mr. Dunford, I know the way." They took the passage to the left, which after a few steps, turned right into a carpeted passageway. Chig could no longer feel the engine.

"Let's stop, Wally."

"But we'll miss the drill, Mr. Dunford." He took a step away. "If the ship goes down, we'll die."

He smiled at Wally's joke. "I guess so. But I'm going back to the cabin." He wanted to maintain civilized relations with Wally. They would share the same living space for one more night. "All right, Wally?"

"We can open one of these." Wally scurried across the carpet to the nearest door, knocked, no answer. He turned the knob and tried to pull, locked. "Maybe there's somebody around who can tell us what to do."

"I'll see you, Wally." Chig started away.

"I'll try this door." He did. It opened.

A deep, rolling, mumbling rumble—he thought of elephants whispering—came from inside the room.

"Huh? Hi. This the boiler room?"

Chig stopped, because the rumble had stopped. "What did they say, Wally?"

"Mr. Dunford? Come here, please. Maybe they'll talk to you."

Chig returned to the door, looked into a room bigger than he had expected, completely padded, walls, ceiling, floors, lit with red bulbs, and hot, packed into its shadows with as many as one hundred Africans chained to the padded floor. Most of the Africans appeared to come from the West Coast. The two nearest the door bore tribal markings. In Europe Chig had seen such markings.

He tried to think of something to say, but could only nod at one of the Africans near the door, brown-skinned, sporting a sparse toothbrush mustache. The African nodded back.

"They don't know anything about a lifeboat drill, Wally."

"Life bode drill?"

Chig moved closer to the African with the mustache. The whites of his eyes looked pink, the pupils dark. "You speak English?"

"Speaking Franch as well, ndugu." He lifted his arm, showed Chig his manacle and chain. "You avez key?"

Chig stepped back, smiled. "But what did you do?"

Eight Africans near the door began to laugh. They all displayed beautiful teeth, straight and bright.

"Sisi for to make slave."

"Excuse me?"

"Come on, Mr. Dunford." Wally stepped in front of him, pulled the door shut. "Don't pay any attention. They can't help us."

20

"CAN'T BE HELPED NEITHER, right?" Of course, he did not believe it. "Thursday you a cold turkey."

"At sundown. Get it? The sun go down and Mrs. Johnson's son go down." He smiled to himself. "But Mrs. Johnson'll live."

Carlyle wondered if he would trust the Devil to keep his word. "For how long?"

"Until she's seventy." Hondo leaned across the table, his eyes too bright. "She on a job with a good pension plan. So at sixty-five she'll retire herself and then have five sick-free years, and by that time she'll be old, and she'll die in her sleep."

Carlyle nodded. "You made that deal with the Devil?"

Hondo picked up his fork. "I don't know why I got rice and peas. I don't like no West Indian food."

"When your mama needed a operation?"

"She did, but no more. Eat, man." He put some rice and peas into his mouth.

"Fool, how you know he'll keep his word? And how you know he haven't make her sick in the first place—if he's the Devil."

Hondo cut into his hamburger steak. "You can trust the Devil; he give results. I seen my Mama dying-sick, and then, jump out the bed." He pointed his fork at Carlyle. "All he did was come to the house and touch her head, and she bouncing on her feet, kissing, hugging me."

"You should've got her a hundred years." He knew he would have tried for more than seventy.

Hondo looked at his plate. "He told me not to waste his time with terms. The man said seventy and I took seventy."

"Finish your food."

They ate, arming against the cold, then decided to walk back to the Grouse for a drink. Snow had begun to fall, sticking. The wind had stopped. They went down the stairs into the toast-warm Grouse, took stools at the bar. In a moment, the barman Nods came to get their order. "Your brother came in looking for you."

Carlyle had left his brother at home, studying African history.

Hondo's spine pulled stiff. "I got two brothers."

"I didn't know that." Nods put a hand on his bar, leaned. "I thought it was just you and Cooley."

"We both got a big brother. What he want?"

"He didn't say."

"Well . . ." Hondo hesitated. "Tell him I was here."

"And Glora's looking for him," Carlyle added. "You want scotch?"

Hondo nodded; they both ordered scotch.

"Why didn't you ask Cooley?"

"She's not his mama; she's mine." He stopped, grunted. "She just raised him. Stepbrother sure stepped on me. He wouldn't give me no money because the doctor said the operation probably wouldn't work. Cooley said he don't gamble. He's cold."

"Ice."

"Hey, man, close that God damn door!"

The door to the Grouse stood open. Snow-carrying wind swept down the steps from the Avenue, gusting cigaret butts toward the rear of the long room.

"Too cold to pull this now. What's wrong with you?" Nods shouted across the bar at the door itself, then stooped, disappeared—stood up on the patron's side. "What's the trouble? Break your hinge?" He grabbed its chrome handle, tried to force it closed.

"Hey, man, cool that chill!"

Nods let go, shrugged, explained to the patrons near him that the door seemed frozen open. "Chicken-hunter sure after Chicken Little tonight. I ain't seen a night this cold since . . ." He looked up the steps, squinting against the wind. "Hey, you a bear?"

It did look like a bear, coming down the stairs, feet appearing first and fur-covered. But after shaggy calves and thighs had passed below the top of the door, the suit's zipper began. Someone wearing a great big baby's snowsuit of fur—a woman of European descent, at least sixty years old, her hair recently curled into tight, blue-white rings—shuffled into the Grouse, and stopped beside Nods. "Hi, Johnny."

"Yes, ma'am." Nods pointed Carlyle's way. "A nice stool at the bar?"

"Stow a stool! Show me a private little booth."

"Hey, Carlyle? Seem like I seen her. She some politician's wife?"

Celebrities from downtown did visit the Grouse. "Maybe. What kind of fur she wearing?"

She passed their backs, cold coming off the damp suit, her curls shining steel-pink in the Grouse's light.

"She do look familiar, Carlyle. Wait a minute."

"I wouldn't wait a second."

"Don't whisper, Johnny. Speak up." She stopped, turned to them. "My ears is just a little bum, but this hearing aid was developed for Arctic use. See?" She pushed her ear, the snail-like aid, into Carlyle's face. She wore good perfume. "I picked it up in Norway just before the expedition sailed."

"Yes, ma'am." He stood up. "It looks like you paid good money for it."

"I didn't pay a thing for it, Johnny."

"You stole it, right, Ma?" He looked at Hondo, snorted.

"Why'd you call me Ma?"

Carlyle smiled. "You remind me of a mother."

"The boys on the expedition called me Ma." She looked at him, her eyes watery and level with his, and showing him her new set of teeth, offered to buy them a drink. "Let me tell you about the expedition, Johnny. We went right to the top of the world. You can't imagine."

She wore mittens of fur—reached out and grabbed his arm, pulled him to the rear of the Grouse, pushed and followed him into a booth. He did not resist; he valued the suit at $250 on the resale.

Hondo sat across from them.

"Now, Johnny, just call me Ma, full name Alice F. Buster." She leaned on him. "I'm an explorer is what they call me. But Ma just wanted to look around."

"What at?" He winked at Hondo. She reminded him of his homeroom teacher the first year after his family had moved from Harlem to the Bronx.

"Now, no making fun of Ma, Johnny. I travelled with the best of them, to the top of the world and back." She talked to him alone, her breath strong, cold and minted.

"To the North Pole?"

She squinted. "What's your name, Johnny?"

"Bedlow." He answered before he realized he did not want to tell. "Juan Bedlow."

"Let me look at you." Her mittens rose to grip his shoulders; he hoped it did not mean an extra trip to the cleaners. "Yes. You look like him."

"Who?" He wondered if the smoke in his brain confused him.

"Your Uncle Wallace."

People still telephoned his house to ask about his uncle, who had sung. "You knew him?"

"Known all the best. I find them and take them on." She released him.

"Is that so?" Carlyle sat up straight. "And you knew my Uncle Wallace?"

"Got close there for a while. In Hollywood." She smiled, not at him. "What a hot one!"

"Yes, ma'am."

She sighed, looked away. "Johnny, I'm awful glad I met up with Wallace's nephew. Makes it a damn sight easier on me." She patted her curls, drew her upper lip away from her teeth. "This hair-do's not me. I just had it done to make me look more modern. The real Ma Buster doesn't pussyfoot around." She stared at him. "I got money and I want a man."

He waited until she looked down at her mittens. "How much money?"

"Outside in my car I got twenty thousand dollars."

She surprised him with the exact figure; he had expected resistance, but it did not matter.

They had not ordered and so just left the Grouse, Ma Buster first, Hondo and Carlyle, climbing the stairs into the fresh snowstorm. Her limousine waited, parked at the corner near Deed's Funeral Home. A chauffer stood in the sole-deep snow ready to open the door.

"Say good-bye to Hondo, Wallace." Ma Buster trudged at his side, had taken his elbow.

"He's going, Ma." Only the money interested him.

"You're horsing me."

"Hey, man?" Hondo stopped walking.

The chauffer bowed, opened the back door.

Hondo fell farther behind them, and Carlyle slowed, waved him closer. "Come on. We riding tonight."

Hondo did not move. The snow falling settled on the bill of his cap. "Hey, man!"

"What?"

"I know where I seen her. The chauffer, man. That's him."

"Who, man?"

"Him."

21

"Wait a minute." He knocked, pressed his ear to the door of the padded room. "Didn't you hear what he said?"

"Sure, Mr. Dunford. But slavery's been abolished for a hundred years. They're probably just criminals, you know, making a joke."

"A joke?" He tried the door, but Wally's slam had tripped the lock. "A joke, Wally?"

"Sure. And we better go before somebody comes. They're probably not allowed visitors." He took Chig's arm. "This way, Mr. Dunford."

They retraced their route to the cabin, Wally leading the way. "It was dirty down there." He opened the cabin door, let Chig pass in. "Did you notice, Mr. Dunford?"

Chig shook his head. "Can I sit on your bed?"

"Sure, Mr. Dunford." Wally began to unbutton his shirt. "I'm changing my clothes. It was real dirty down there."

Chig pulled the sheet over Wally's rumpled bunk, and sat down. "I'll wait until you leave, then I'll get ready for my date." He hoped Wally would catch his hint. "All right?"

"Huh? Sure, Mr. Dunford." He kicked off his loafers, changed from chino pants to faded blue jeans, buttoned his fly. "I got it. They're sailors who mutinied." He smiled. "Sailors still mutiny, Mr. Dunford. We used to read about them in current events class."

"But when did they mutiny?"

Wally ran the thick end of his comb through his red hair. "Probably a couple days ago."

"Before we got on the ship?"

"Sure, Mr. Dunford. Why else are they locked up?"

"But didn't you hear . . ." He stopped to wonder if he had actually heard the words. He had fears concerning his hearing. "He said they were slaves. At least that's what I think he said. I mean, meant."

"Ya. Maybe that's what you mean, Mr. Dunford. I saw that happen before." He nodded his head. "We don't like to think about it, but mutineers and people like that are still going around." He rolled up the sleeves of his clean, pale-blue button-down shirt, stuffed a handkerchief into his back pocket, snapped to attention. "Well, I'm ready to go. Do I look all right?"

Wally's question surprised him, but Chig looked him over, found the handkerchief protruding, pointed.

"Thanks, Mr. Dunford." Wally patted all his pockets. "You know, it may sound funny, but sharing this cabin with you has really hit the nail on the head far as my TYO Team Year in Europe is concerned." He rocked from foot to foot. "And thanks for helping me with Lynn."

"But I don't think I—"

"For talking to her, Mr. Dunford. I knew she'd respect your opinion. You were swell."

Chig accepted the compliment without comment, and Wally, his freckles stretched into a smile, left him alone to realize again that he and Wendy were on the same ship. Could he accomplish anything before they reached New York? What did he want to accomplish? He thought about that question a long while, remembered himself searching Europe for her and decided finally that he wanted to marry her. That was his dream; he wanted to marry—Wendy.

"Wally? Wally? I know you're in there!" The man began to pound the door, and shout over the sound of his fist. "Come on, Wally! Open up and meet your fate!"

Chig opened the door.

"Lookout, huh?" He pushed his way into the cabin, a boyish face on a large body. "Where's Wally? I'm Oglethrope."

"Nice to meet you, Mr. Oglethrope." Chig smiled from the door. "He just left. You lead the tour he's on, don't you?" The name Oglethrope had made him imagine an older, thinner face.

"Bull's-eye." He patted the upper bunk. "This Wally's?"

Chig indicated the lower. "My name—"

"He been in it every night so far?"

"I think so. Would you like to leave a note for him?"

"If you want to know the truth, bud, I thought I'd find them right here." He patted Chig's bunk again. "Going sneakers."

"Excuse me?"

"The both of them. Sneakers." He hammered one fist into the other palm. "I better not catch them, all I can say." He nodded his head, vowing, took a deep breath. "Not that I mind personally. I'm not blanketyblank prude."

Chig nodded.

Oglethrope frowned. "Going sneakers like that. They signed up knowing the rules. And the rules say no mixing between the sexes."

Chig tried a question. "You mean like talking?"

Oglethrope cocked his head. "You don't know about TYO Team Tours, do you."

He shook his head. "I've been in Europe, I guess."

"You guess." Oglethrope rested his shoulder against the upper bunk's side. "How long do you guess you were there?"

"Eight years." He thought, added, "But I was going back and forth. But I think I'm going back for good now."

"And tell me, bud, how did you make the money to do this?"

"Scholarships. I was a student."

"For eight years?" Oglethrope reddened. "Listen, if you want some friendly advice, you look like a guy at loose ends. When you get to New York, get in touch with your nearest TYO Team Organizer. She could really help you."

"Excuse me, Mr. Oglethrope, but before I could join TYO, I mean, I'd have to know more about it." He laughed. "I might not even qualify for membership."

"Don't worry, bud. We're not like those Eastern clubs. You can join if you get the right frame of mind." Oglethrope's chest expanded under his open-necked dull-yellow sportshirt. He sat on the lower bunk, on Wally's pillow. "Come here."

Chig did not know how to ask Oglethrope to leave. He stepped away from the door, but left it open.

"Come here," Oglethrope ordered again. "Do I look funny to you?"

Chig shook his head.

"At one time, I used to go sneakers, just like them. I was an athlete, you see. I got three pro offers." He stared up, his gray eyes flat. Around his neck on a metal chain hung an acorn. "The night we beat the team from Clearwater, Jerry Orloch bet me five hundred dollars I wouldn't pull out my eye. Well, there was a lot of booze around that night, and I was kidding and he was kidding, but when I started I said to myself, stop when it starts to hurt. But it never did start to hurt." He reached into his face, fingered his left gray eye out of its socket. "They had to stop me. See for yourself."

"Yes. I . . ."

Oglethrope replaced his eye, went on: "I learned something that night. I was at the bottom of the tree. Wrecked my whole future in sport. The scouts didn't come around anymore." He lowered his head. "You might think it shames me to tell you something like that, but it doesn't. I get stronger every time I tell it. I know I crashed through with TYO."

Chig nodded. "I guess so."

"TYO has representatives in all the hospitals, little women to mend the men and send them back to battle." He laughed. "The Rep at Gully City General was a little cutie of about five foot three. Today that little cutie is called Mrs. Oglethrope."

"Oh?" For some reason—perhaps Wally had suggested it—Chig had believed Oglethrope an unmarried man. "Is she with the tour?"

"Not on your life. She's home with my brother, running the store, hardware." He paused, found his place. "You see, TYO taught me that some things are more important than money. Like devotion to duty and sacrifice. Look at all our famous men and the thing that marks them is how much they sacrifice. TYO gave me that. And it can give it to you too." He put his hands on his knees, pushed himself to his feet. "Do me a favor."

"If I can, Mr. Oglethrope."

"Keep an eye on those kids for me." He looked for, found the open door. "Let me know if you see anything that smells fishy."

Chig thought he understood, but wanted to make certain. "What do you mean by fishy, Mr. Oglethrope?"

"Come on, bud. We're all grown-ups here." Oglethrope scolded, winking his left eye. "Just look into Wally's mug, watch him walk. The kid's face is a raspberry bush." He took Chig's arm, guided him toward the door. "Let me have a report at dinner."

"If I see anything." Chig waved good-bye, shut and locked the door, looked at his watch. If he did not hurry, he would arrive late for his date.

He stripped to his skin, checked his chin, finding that his shave would last another day, then washed and deodorized himself. He decided to wear his gray summer suit, a white short-sleeved shirt and a dark wool tie. The result did not excite him. He had not aimed for excitement, rather for a certain scholarly solidity, the appearance of a man who taught Comparative Literature at a small Eastern college for $9,000 a year.

Wendy waited, a queen in the center of a curving corner seat, when he stepped over the doorsill of the third-class lounge. Her smile lit his way through the tables separating them; he did not mind that some old ladies tucked their cards to their bosoms and pinched their brows, watching him and Wendy meet.

"Chig. How are you?" She raised her chin, offered her hand the moment his thighs bumped her table.

"Hello, Wendy." He took her long, soft hand. "I'm fine." He wanted to add the word: now, but could not.

"Do sit down, and tell me what you've done." She had taken up her hair, knit it into a large soft black bun. She wore a neat tweed suit, white blouse, bunches of silk at the collar. "Please do."

He slid into the seat beside her, feeling the beat of his heart in his temples. "There's not much—" He cut himself off, made himself look into her eyes. "I'm very happy to see you."

She seemed surprised, blinked once, looked away. "That's very kind, Chig."

He wanted to repeat himself and make her understand all he had tried to say, but the right moment slipped by and instead, he asked where she had spent the year.

"In Africa." Her face did not move.

"North Africa?" People did sometimes take the boat over from the Spanish Islands, or Sicily.

She smiled. "No. Central Africa."

He nodded. "That sounds like a nice trip."

"Yes, it was."

He turned toward the bar. He would have to go fetch their drinks, but wanted to waste no time waiting. The bar steward stood idle, but Chig did not leave her. "I bet you got a lot of sun."

"It was wonderful. Noon for twelve hours each day." She straightened her back. "And you stayed in Europe?"

"Yes. But I travelled around . . ."

She closed her eyes, opened them. "I suppose you'll say you were tracking me down."

"In a way."

She sucked her tongue. "Well, why don't you really tell me that?"

"Excuse me?"

"I asked you why don't you tell me you searched for me all over Europe? I might like that."

The crystal of his watch needed tightening. "Yes. Wendy. I was looking for you."

"Dear Chig, you haven't found me yet."

"Why did you leave like that, Wendy?"

"Because you took too long."

22

"Not him." He inspected the chauffer, a little man with bowed legs on black shoes, dark wool car-coat over a barrel stomach, a round Southern European face under a black cap with a shiny water-beaded visor. Carlyle could not see the chauffer's eyes in the shadows, through the falling snow. "Come here, Hondo."

In the middle of the sidewalk, dancing from one foot to the other, Hondo shook his head. "I already made my appointment."

"What's wrong with him?" Ma Buster still clung to his arm, smiled from her furs. "Well? We want privacy, don't we?"

"Wait a minute." Carlyle pulled himself free, and stepped closer to Hondo, realizing his friend felt afraid. "That's the Devil?"

Hondo nodded. "Only last time he had on a silk suit."

"He don't look like the Devil to me."

"He don't look like the Devil to me neither."

Carlyle thought for a moment, shrugged. "So what."

"So what!" Hondo made the face of a burp.

"Far as I see, he's a chauffer."

"But he's the Devil."

"Okay, but you already signed up. So what you worrying about?"

They climbed into the back of the limousine, Ma Buster between them, pounding both their knees with mittened fists. "I can't say I'm happy to have you aboard, Johnny, but Wallace and me'll make out." She turned to him. "Catch my drift?"

"Easy, Ma." He removed her mitten from his leg. "First, show me that money you talking about."

She smiled with her upper lip, removed the fur from her right hand, unzipped the suit, reached in and pulled up a pouch-like purse.

"You see that, Hondo?" He had caught her in a lie. "She told us it was in the car."

Hondo's whites shone at him from the backseat's far corner. "I see it."

He studied Ma Buster's large, square, weathered, human face. "Listen, Ma, I don't know how they act where you come from, but now you in Harlem where the woman chase the man, until she gets selected to get caught." Cooley used this approach with women of European descent. "If you don't like it, well . . ."

Hondo forced himself to laugh. Carlyle reached across Ma Buster and let his friend slap his palm.

Ma Buster did not laugh. "You wanted to see my money?"

"We ain't laughing at you, Ma." He took the pouch from her lap. For a minute, the lock would not work. When he did open it, he found the money she had mentioned, and a checkbook besides. He counted himself one hundred dollars in tens, returned the purse, patted her bare hand. "Keep that, Ma." He smiled. "You know, I'm not only interested in your money. A lot of women with money I don't mess with."

"Don't horse me." She straightened up, breathed through her nose. "Ma's seen your type before."

He answered softly. "You never met nobody like me, Ma."

"What about your uncle?"

But she had called him Wallace. "You met him in Hollywood, right? When, fifty-six?"

"Stow fifty-six. September fifty-seven."

"Maybe so." He sat up straight. "Tell him to drive us to City Island." He wanted to take her into the Bronx somewhere.

"Aye!" She leaned forward, tapped on the glass separating them from the chauffer. Before she spoke the order, the chauffer cut the limousine across traffic, into and out of a U-turn around the divider, sending them north on the Avenue.

The chauffer could hear them. "Open that glass, Ma."

Ma Buster pressed a button; the glass slid open.

"Listen, man: Drive Careful."

"Yes, sir." The chauffer kept his eyes on the Avenue and the double-parked cars. He looked human, his ears pink and round as roses, lobeless.

"Remember because I could get you fired."

"Yes, sir."

Carlyle sat back, smiled at Ma Buster. "Just steadying the ship, Ma." He enjoyed riding in good cars, especially if he did not have to drive. "We'll have us a good time, Ma. We'll get some fried clams and fries and have a little party, just the three of us, and him too, if he wants." He indicated the chauffer. "Then we'll drop off Hondo and send your man home, and have a little party, just us." He winked.

She winked in return, but her face did not change. He wondered if he had taken the right trail to Ma Buster's heart. "What's wrong, Ma?"

She lowered her chin to her fur-covered breast. "Ma ain't happy." She laughed, howling at the upholstered roof. "I got money and I want a man is what the old gal said."

He relaxed. "You said you didn't pussyfoot around."

"That's a snort coming from Ma Buster. I bark like I got a hell of a bite." The whites of her eyes islanded their light-gray pupils. "Ma Buster's a virgin. Spent the whole sledge-ride with men and not one of them ever laid a mitt on me."

"That's too bad." He looked out of the window. They had just passed the last barbecue place before the bridge into the Bronx. "Why you think that happened?"

"Just turn your goggles on me."

He set his face, looked at her, smiled. "You got one little thing going for you."

"I do?"

He nodded. "Money."

"You think that was enough to get Ma banged?"

"Works most of the time."

"But I was saving myself for the right guy." She sighed. "The pay-off didn't come until after the expedition and by that time, my looks was gone. Too much hard living with the boys."

"That's a shame, Ma." He clicked his tongue.

"Just my card. I was never known as one of Gully City's prettiest."

"You don't understand, Ma. The shame be that nobody climbed in your bed and took you off all them long nights. Right, Hondo?"

Hondo nodded.

"But they all acted like real gentlemen, and I always tried to fit right in and not use my sex. That's what I wanted to show, that a girl could do anything and they didn't have to pack special equipment."

"How many men went up, Ma?"

"Set out with fourteen." She paused. "Came back with twelve."

"How long all this take?"

"You see, it was off and on, three years."

"Three years? I don't care what you look like, Ma. One of them should've got over. I mean, you're a woman."

"Stow that. I tried not to be."

"Quite enough, Miss Buster." The partition separating the front where the chauffer sat from the backseat began without squeak or scrape to slide down into the floor. "Say no more." The chauffer let go his wheel, swiveled to face them. "His main concern is the money."

Guiding itself, the limousine approached an overpass with a slow curve beyond it—rolling away from City Island and north into Westchester.

The chauffer shook his head. "You've missed his heart by miles, Miss Buster."

"Now, didn't I tell you it was him!" Hondo twisted up his face. "I'll haunt you, man."

Their self-steering limousine did not impress him. If he waited in the right downtown places, he might see another just like it. "Wait a minute, Hondo."

"We are he, Mr. Bedlow." Perhaps because of the bad light from the lamps down the center-strip snapping by, the chauffer's eyes seemed dull-yellow. "And there's absolutely nothing you can get from us without giving something in return. We believe in simple transactions."

Carlyle nodded. "And you looking to buy my soul."

"Yours especially, Mr. Bedlow."

Carlyle turned to Hondo. "You went for this game?"

"Don't forget my mama." Hondo shivered; though the limousine owned a good heating system, his teeth rattled.

"Man, I never seen her." He wanted to get out now, to call it even with the hundred he carried in his pocket. "I didn't see her get sick and I didn't see him get her well."

"Trust your friend's word, Mr. Bedlow."

He looked hard at the chauffer, tried to decide if he might carry a gun. "So what game you really running?"

"Join us and see. We have room for you on our team." His brittle voice did not fit his heavy face.

"Buying souls?" Carlyle laughed once. "I don't need no souls."

"We also offer money, women, glamourous apartments, the finest wardrobes. Your assignment would be signing on your friends. Your payment would be the world."

"Starting with Ma?"

"You'd be surprised at the material of which Miss Buster is composed."

Carlyle shook his head. "I don't believe I would. Listen, man, can you stop this thing too?" He wanted to get out before they remembered their money.

"Apprehensive, Mr. Bedlow?"

"Tired. Drop us at a subway, will you?"

"A subway, is it?" The chauffer pressed one of a row of buttons on the steering post. The limousine left the highway climbing the next exit ramp, came to a full stop, turned right. Carlyle promised himself to own a limousine like it someday.

"We see that our car pleases you, Mr. Bedlow."

"Sure do, boss. You have to tell me where you bought it at."

The limousine stopped beside a small grove of oak trees. They were in one of the residential areas of Westchester, the houses back from the street, each on its own acre.

"Your subway, Mr. Bedlow."

"Good. Thanks. The man's making us walk, Hondo." He opened the door, climbed out, in a moment saw Hondo's head across the roof. He leaned back inside. "You owe me a pair of shoes, devil." His feet already felt wet in the cuff-deep snow.

The chauffer raised a pistol, pointed it at Carlyle's face. "You owe me one hundred dollars, Mr. Bedlow."

23

"Excuse me?" She had seemed to like him to go slow. "I mean, what did I take too long to do?"

She shook her head, sighed, looked at him, shook her head again. "How old are you, Chig?"

"Twenty-nine." He wondered whether she would find him too old, or too young. "I'll be thirty next month."

She nodded. "Why don't you get us some sherry. Please."

He fled to the bar—waiting for the bar steward to hand him the stemmed glasses, tried to decide what he would talk about when he returned to her. Each topic led to marriage, and in his mind, the proposal offended her.

A glass in each hand, he passed back among the tables. The old ladies, brows of shiny dark hair, still watched. Some had stopped playing cards altogether.

He sat down across from her.

"Look at me, Chig."

"Sure, Wendy." But he could not keep himself from inspecting the wall behind her, could not meet her stare.

"You're unlike any Colored I've ever met."

He had to look back at her now. "Is that so?" They had spoken of the Experience before, but never with specific reference to Chig. "I can think of at least two others." His brother, his sister.

"Perhaps." She smiled, her dimple coming to her chin. "But I believe you're perfect."

"Tell that to my mother."

"I feel sure she already knows."

He listened to the warmth come to her upper-class Virginian voice, shrugged. "Everybody's disappointed in me, but all for different reasons, including me. I can't seem to get oriented." He used his mother's sentence. "I've been . . . peripatetic for eight years now."

"But, Chig, why?"

He paused to listen to her soft voice, again, inside his ear. "There doesn't seem to be a place for me; there . . . I don't know. Once I thought I'd be a lawyer."

"My father's a lawyer. He—" She stopped herself. "But I won't talk about him." She smiled. "But I want to." She reached out and took his hand. "I do like you, Chig. So until we get to New York, let's pretend we're not us."

"Excuse me?"

They finished their sherry. Then she pulled him to his feet, led him to walk the deck, as the sun began to ease down toward the edge of the dark sea. She held his hand, squeezed it when the wind blew. "You should go to Africa someday, Chig."

"Would I like it?"

"You'd love it. The girls are beautiful. They'd teach you important things about yourself."

His comment came too slowly; he decided to try to change the subject slightly. "There are some Africans on this boat."

"There are?" She let go his hand too quickly. "From where?"

"The West Coast, probably." He did not really want to talk

about Africans at all. "One said he spoke French, I think he said."

She inspected him from his shoes to his hair. Perhaps he should have used his stocking-cap. He could not remember her ever looking at him so carefully, frankly staring at him.

"Are you really the person you seem, Chig?" Before he could ask what she meant, she continued. "But if you weren't, would you tell me?"

"Tell you I was—"

"A big, fat acorn." She poked out her lips, and bugged her eyes.

"A what?" He laughed, enjoyed feeling how nice it felt to laugh. When he finished, he asked her if it were possible for him to be an acorn.

"Haven't you seen any on the ship?"

He had, somewhere. "All over the place."

She smiled at him, a quiet smile between them, and the sea wind around them. "I know you have. But since you're on our side, it doesn't matter."

"It doesn't?"

"No, dear-Chig." She kissed his cheek, hugged his arm. "But please go on about those Africans."

"Well, there's not much more . . ."

She pulled it out of him, helped him to unburden himself; the Africans disturbed him. "I mean, I know Wally's answer makes sense. That would explain the chains. But if they mutinied, wouldn't the ship seem different? More unsettled? Anything strange happening up in first class?"

She shook her head.

He kept talking: "You understand? The ship's normal, not like a hundred African sailors just tried to take it over. I admit, this is only my second time on an Atlantic ship, but everything seems . . . normal. Besides, one African said he was coming for to be a slave. Something like that. At any rate, what do you suppose happened?"

"The chains are the riddle, isn't that right?" She half-smiled.

"That's what I think. But . . ." He hesitated, knowing what he wanted to confess might lower her estimation of him. "But I'm not sure he said it, because I'm a little worried about my hearing."

"Oh, Chig, that's not true."

"I don't know. People say things to me, and I don't understand them. Or what I hear doesn't make any sense."

"Do I make sense to you?"

He laughed away his embarrassment, then decided to act bravely. "You make perfect sense to me, Wendy."

"For goodness sakes, Chig, don't be so serious." He could see nothing on her face except her tan. "You make me nervous."

"But, Wendy . . ."

She watched the sea, her back to the setting sun. "Let me be very clear, Chig. I will never marry you."

"But, why? Why can't you marry me?" Even in the wind, his voice grew too loud. "I mean, if you want to. You seem to like me. I don't want to get married on shipboard or anything."

"You're spoiling it. I just could never marry you. That's all." She knit her hands, looked at them.

"It's race." He shook his head. "God, isn't that stupid."

"It is not race. Race does not exist. If anything, it's culture." She blinked, then closed her eyes tight, began to speak before she opened them again. "Don't think I'm stupid because my skin is white. It goes deeper than skin. I have relationships I shouldn't like to give up, places I go where you could not go. Race? It's ancest—"

He cut her off quite deliberately. "But why don't we forget that and find out what we have as people?"

"All right. But you still can't think you can marry me, Chig.

Must I tell you everything?" She took a breath. "I'm not travelling alone. But until tomorrow afternoon, we can pretend."

He knew she had made her final offer. He frowned, nodded.

"Now cheer up." She scolded him, then laughed. "Let me show you the real me, almost."

He smiled, and in five more minutes, she had convinced him it would be great fun to talk to the Africans chained in the padded room.

"But what'll we talk about?" He followed her down a narrow, curving staircase they had found, listened to her heels on uncovered steel.

"About why they're chained up." Her part ran straight and tan from forehead to bun.

"Why should they tell us?"

"Why shouldn't they?" She turned, smiled up at him.

They went deeper into the ship, came finally, from a new direction, into the carpeted passageway where Wally had opened the door. But the door remained locked. Wendy put her ear to it. "I can't hear a thing."

He stood behind her. "It's completely padded." He felt his heart flutter as he spoke. "I think we should get out of here."

"But we haven't solved the riddle of the chains, Dr. Dunford." She made her voice very English. "And I have reason to believe these waters are troubled."

"Now just suppose they really are, you know, slaves."

"We shall have to set them free, Dr. Dunford."

That stopped him. He realized that even as she joked, she had given one possible answer. "Well, let's hope Wally's right then."

"You're afraid." She stepped into the middle of the passageway, counted the doors.

"If they are slaves, the whole crew knows about it, which means that even if we did something, it wouldn't work."

She sucked her tongue. "Don't be dreary, Chig. Besides, we haven't proved a thing yet." The second door she tried moved, swung open into a room not much wider than the door, but deep, furnished with a desk and two captain's chairs with doweled backs.

Wendy walked in. "Isn't this an enchanting little room!" She went all the way to the cabin's porthole, came partway back. "Come in and shut the door. We'll pretend it's ours."

He sighed, certain trouble waited, entered the cabin and closed the door. "Let's not stay too long, all right?"

She bent to look at books and papers on the desk. He joined her, patted her shoulder lightly. "Don't touch anything, Wendy."

She picked up a small slim book on losing weight, complete with calo-chart, and then another on games for the bedridden. Chig grew interested in a paperback on isometric exercises.

Under a cross-section of a limb of lacquered oak used as a paperweight, they found a stack of business-machine paper, its sides calibrated like film, a long list of words and numbers:

SL2,220,101/A22/GARDENER/6499.95
SL2,220,102/A47/COOK/5999.00
SL2,220,103/A34/SHOEMAKER/7399.99
SL2,220,104/A33/BARBER/4990.00
SL2,220,105/A42/POTTER/7444.95
SL2,220,106/A29. . . . . . .

He stopped reading; he had found trouble enough. The Africans were slaves, an even one hundred of them.

24

"WHAT HUNDRED?" If Carlyle spoke to the real Devil, and the real Devil wanted to buy his soul, he would not shoot him in Westchester.

"Miss Buster's hundred, please." The chauffer waved his pistol under Carlyle's nostrils.

"What about my shoes, Mr. Good Deal?"

Hondo watched through the opposite window. "Remember my mama, and give the man the money, man."

"Very good, Mr. Johnson." The chauffer nodded. "And if you do feel abused, Mr. Bedlow, keep fifty dollars."

Carlyle reached for the money, peeled off and repocketed five tens, handed the difference to the chauffer. "Fair's fair, you understand." He backed out of the car, stood up in the still, cold, blue air.

"I understand, Mr. Bedlow." The doors closed. Ma Buster waved from her place; the chauffer's voice continued over a public address system. "Fear's fear. Until Thursday, Mr. Johnson." The limousine did not give off exhaust, just moved, designing the fresh snow with row after row of tiny interlaced hammers, its tail-end, finally, becoming part of the shadows.

They stood alone, their warm shoes melting the snow. Halfway to the corner, a globe on an old lampstand, a living-room light out of doors, glowed yellow amid snow-rounded trees. Hondo shivered, his shoulders pinching his ears, bit his lips.

"What you so tightened up about? You just made twenty-five dollars."

He watched Hondo lower his head and hurl it at Carlyle's stomach, embracing Carlyle's hips, tossing him back into a snowbank. He could think but could not move enough to avoid Hondo's fists—balled, the size of brown melons—pounding his cheeks. He could talk now, in a few seconds would fight back. "Hey, Hondo. You messing with Carlyle. I can whip—"

"Here I am." Hondo hit him again, on the nose.

He could not see. "If you want a fight, man, let's whip shit out a him." He tasted the blood from his nose.

"Awh, man . . ." His eyes returned: Hondo shook his head. "You crazy." He stood up. "Talking about whipping shit out the Devil."

Carlyle sat up. "Look at you calling me crazy!" He wiped his face with his hand, bloodying his palm, then covered his nose with snow.

Hondo started to laugh. "You look like a crazy, psychopathetic rooster, nigger."

Carlyle threw away the red snow ball, felt his hair, ruined, sticking straight out from his head. He stood up. "He running a game on you."

"For what?" Hondo clapped his hands, shrugged. "I didn't give him no money. In fact, he gave me cab fare home after I signed up."

"Maybe he haven't sprung the whole trick yet."

Hondo sucked his tongue. "He'll spring the whole trick on Thursday when I die."

Carlyle shook his head. "Wait until Friday before you sure."

Hondo started to wilt, his shoulders dropping. "Let's forget it. The man's the Devil and Thursday I die, and if you ain't messed my deal, my mama'll live sick-free for the next twenty years." He started away.

Carlyle caught up, grabbed Hondo's shoulder. "I'll tell you, man. I'll lead your mama away from your grave."

"Won't be no grave." Hondo shook himself free, slid his hands into his overcoat pockets. "I'm supposed to meet him at his office. Then we go somewhere else. I don't think I'll be a body after that."

"So you told her you dying Thursday?"

"And give her a shock? She haven't been well that long."

Carlyle stopped, sighed, hurried to catch up again. "And you think she won't get sick wondering why you didn't come home and filling out a missing-persons and waiting for news when they drag the river?"

"It's my mama." They arrived at the corner, paused without word to decide which way to go. "But maybe I should tell her I'm taking a long trip, like to California. Michael went out there. And I think his sister went out there too."

"Little, short Michael?" From the intersection all the streets looked the same, globes diminishing away to yellow dots.

"He got big." Hondo turned a slow circle in place. "Which way we going?"

Carlyle shrugged; one of his shoulders pained him. "I ain't been here before."

"Listen, Carlyle, do me a favor."

Carlyle nodded, waited.

"If I write a letter telling my mama I'm in California, will you send it to Michael and ask him to send it to her? For the postmark?"

"Sure. If you die." He coughed, watched the steam. "But who'll tell her you dead?"

Before Hondo could answer, the truck came, braked, a bright green pickup truck, its back filled with ladders and cans of paint.

"You men lost?" The driver occupied at least half the cab's seat. He wore a leather aviator's jacket with a lambskin collar, a flat black leather cap. "You men lost."

"We got mugged." Carlyle explained his face, stepped up to the window. "Where we at?"

"Brother, I could never tell you. Get in."

They walked around the truck, waited for the driver to open the door. Carlyle let Hondo climb in first. He pulled shut the door, cramping the cab. "You lost too?"

The driver shook his head. "I just don't know the name, but I know the place. One town end; one start. I haven't get a interest in them kinds of signs." He indicated a card-holder on the metal dashboard, shifted into gear.

Carlyle took a card:

BUBBAH'S SIGNS
ALL KINDS

RIChland 161

"This you?"

"No. I'm giving some other man's cards away. Yes, man. That's me." He extended his hand to them, Hondo then Carlyle. "Where you heading?"

"The city."

"I'll take you to the end of the line." Bubbah's smooth, black, fat face hid his age.

"Thanks. You a painter or something?"

Bubbah shook his head. "I paint signs. For money." He smiled. "But they good signs anyway."

"Carlyle? Excuse me, man." Hondo pulled Carlyle's coat sleeve. "Suppose you write a letter in about two months and say you my friend in California. You know, using another name, and tell her I got killed, eat up by sharks, and leaving no remains. But you seen it. She don't know your writing. And you send that to Michael."

"Taking a trip, brother?"

Carlyle answered. "He trying to cut some people loose." He looked deep into Hondo's eyes, made sure he understood. "Sure. I could do that. But that still some shock for a girl who just got well."

Hondo did not comment.

"But he ain't really visiting California." Bubbah came to a full stop, looked both ways, went on straight.

"No." He decided to risk telling more. Bubbah seemed experienced, might have seen a game like this before. "Some devil have him in a trick."

"What kind?"

"Not about money. They just seem to want his body."

"You mean like a guinea pig?"

"Hear him, Hondo? Maybe they'll pickle you. I seen a cat in a big bottle in the museum once."

Bubbah did not agree. "No money in that. Five hundred at the most. But if he got relations, remember the ransom."

"You listening?"

Hondo nodded. "She have saved a dollar a week for the last twenty-six years, never took out a cent. She wouldn't even go for it when she got sick. She call it her funeral money."

"So you mixed up with some old girl." Bubbah's laugh rumbled.

"Old enough to be his mama." Carlyle smiled. "Thursday night she'll get a phone call, somebody talking about he's safe, Mrs. Johnson, but drop a paper bag at a bridge in Bronxville."

Hondo shook his head. "She won't get no phone call."

Carlyle leaned close to Hondo's ear. "We waste him?"

"Sure." But the idea did not make him happy.

They reached a road, two lanes winding through parks and thickets of snow-clogged trees. The road turned into a highway; the private homes changed to apartment buildings. They left the highway, made two lefts, and started to climb a long hill, passing several stranded automobiles. The elevated subway ran along the ridge of the hill.

"We live right near here, Bubbah. Drop us anywhere."

"I'll take you home." He carried them to Carlyle's house, looked down at them from his window. "Don't do nothing foolish."

Hondo seemed tired. "Thanks for the ride, Bubbah."

"Later, man."

"Just do what you ken." Bubbah raced the motor, shifted, moved off, ladders and cans rattling.

Carlyle felt for his keys. "I don't think we can kill him. We don't have no organization to back us up. But we can give him a cheek-scar, hope it teach him a lesson. You hungry?"

"Just how you plan to scar the Devil? Acid in his face?"

"The Devil? I thought you said—"

"I did. Before I remembered how sick my mama got."

25

"WHAT DO YOU THINK NOW, my good doctor?"

He thought he felt sick, then realized he felt fear. "That you should put that down and we should go—all right?"

"Yes. But first we'll collect some evidence."

"There's plenty across the hall." His joke made him sad. "Come on, Wendy." He grabbed her wrist, took the slave manifest from her, and put it on the desk.

When he released her, she picked it up again, tore out a page, folded it small and stuffed it into her purse. "All right, now."

He backed away from the desk, toward the door, found the knob with his hand. "I guess we better just walk out, and if we run into anyone, pretend we're lost."

"All right, doctor."

He opened the door a crack and spied Oglethrope loitering in the passageway. He took a breath, stepped out. "Hello, sir. Which way is it to the infirmary?"

"The infirmary, bud?" Oglethrope rounded his right eye. "Who's hurting?"

"A woman's problem." Wendy raised her chin, offered her hand, introduced herself.

"A prize to meet you, Miss Whitman." Oglethrope squinted, it seemed, at her breasts. "You got family in the Midwest?"

"This is Mr. Oglethrope," Chig interjected, taking her elbow. "Feeling all right, Miss Whitman?"

She nodded, watching Oglethrope. "I have family everywhere. We all haven't remained in Virginia."

"Virginia, huh?" He looked at Chig. "Maybe you don't need TYO after all."

"Do you know where the infirmary is, sir?" He tried to keep his face from moving.

Oglethrope pointed. "To the end of the passage, make a right and climb the stairs. And take it slow for the little lady's sake."

"Thanks a lot, Mr. Oglethrope." He squeezed her elbow. "Come on, Miss Whitman." He pulled her gently.

"I'm sure I'm going to see you before the end of the voyage, Mr. Oglethrope." She turned back, smiled a good-bye that looked to Chig like a hello.

Oglethrope did not answer; his eye watched them until they turned the corner, kept them silent until they regained the deck, dark now, the wind stopped, the waves calmed.

"He's so muscular. Is your friend an athlete?"

"I think so. I don't know him very well." He tried to order his thoughts, did not have time for Oglethrope. "What do we do now?"

He could not see her face clearly.

"About those Africans, you mean?"

"Yes." The moon had not yet risen. "The slaves."

"But, Chig-dear, they're not slaves."

He closed his eyes against the dark shadows, and found more. "No?"

"Certainly not. They're just plain Africans." She paused. "It's an interesting idea, but . . ."

"What about your evidence?"

"What's wrong with you, Chig? I didn't say evidence. I said momento."

As his eyes grew accustomed to the dark, her face came up, mouth stretched wide but unsmiling. If he did not steer himself away from it, they would argue. Besides, she did not have to believe it. "All right, they're just plain Africans." He reached for her hand.

"Nigger? Don't you dare touch me! Unless I give you my expressed permission."

Wow. Again, it came to that. It always seemed to come to that. He sighed, backed away. "I hope you and your friend have a pleasant voyage, Wendy."

"Don't pretend to be so God-awful polite." Her voice stayed dry, even, perfect.

"I'm not pretending. We house-niggers are bred to be polite." He even attempted a little bow, felt foolish, did not care. Walking away, he wondered whether she watched after him, but did not look back.

"Wow," he said aloud to himself, still walking, shaking his head. The nigger had hid behind all the words all that time. He simply never wanted to hear or see it, just as he did not want to believe he had bought passage on a slave ship.

But then, perhaps the Africans had signed on of their own free will, as bond-slaves. They might not even land in the United States, might sail on after he had disembarked.

He heard steps, thought they would pass him by. "You're late for supper, Mr. Dunford."

"I'm a little overweight anyway, Wally."

"Huh?" He wore a plaid sport coat over his blue shirt, and a tie.

"I'm only joking, Wally." He tried to smile, could not.

"Ya. Sure. I asked, Mr. Dunford, and they said you didn't have to sit at your assigned table on the last night, so I saved you a place."

"Thanks anyway, Wally. I'm not hungry."

"You have to eat, Mr. Dunford." He wrinkled his nose. "You paid."

"You may be right, Wally." He pretended seriousness. "Let's go to dinner."

They went inside through the lounge, brightly lit and empty, and one level down, entered the dining room, ringing with heavy forks on heavy plates. Lynn and Oglethrope had already taken two places at Wally's table.

Oglethrope grabbed his napkin from his lap, stood up. "Glad you came along, bud." He extended his hand.

"So am I, Mr. Oglethrope." He shook the hand once, let go. "How are you, Lynn?"

"You know Lynn, bud?"

She smiled. "Fine, thanks."

Wally took the seat across from Lynn at the small square table. Chig sat down, facing Oglethrope.

"Want some bread, bud?"

"Yes, thanks." He took the plate, remembering he had met Oglethrope near the slave-quarters. "Did Mr. Oglethrope tell you he was looking for you, Wally?"

Wally nodded, his head down, fork chasing peas.

"Found him too. Both of them." Oglethrope had finished eating, only a paste of gravy and mashed potatoes smearing his plate. "Going sneakers never pays."

Chig looked at his food, picked up his silverware. "What kind of meat—"

"Roast pig." Oglethrope's lips had not moved. "Some nice-looking girl you picked up, bud."

He felt his stomach shift, caught it. "Isn't she, Mr. Oglethrope?" Let him believe what he wanted to believe.

"He knew her from before. Right, Mr. Dunford?"

"Just a second, Wally." He made himself smile. "Pardon me for asking, Mr. Oglethrope, can they talk? I mean, to each other?"

Oglethrope curled his lip. "Let them try."

Chig gave the man his nervous little laugh. "I just wanted to know. So I wouldn't make a mistake."

Oglethrope blinked. "You're a cool one, Dunford."

"I am?"

"You think I don't know you were helping them go sneakers?" He inhaled through his nose. "You folks always meddle."

"Excuse me?" He began to worry about the small bones in his ears, then remembered Wendy. "Meddle in what, Mr. Oglethrope?"

Oglethrope made the motion of pounding the table, but pulled his punch, attracting no attention. "In people's private lives." He glared at Chig, then Wally, and finally Lynn. His face softened. "Can't really blame the kids. Not with folks like you around to ruin their outlook."

Chig drew a deep breath. "Mr. Oglethrope, I don't understand what you're talking about."

"You don't?" Oglethrope held his butter knife in his right hand.

"It's all right, Mr. Dunford. He's right." Wally's face puckered. "I mean about me and Lynn."

His left leg itched, tickled. He reached to scratch and felt the point of a folded slip of paper. Lynn stared at Oglethrope. He took her note. "About what, Wally?"

"He really didn't help us, Mr. Oglethrope." A whine came into Wally's voice. "We did it ourselves."

"Dunford knows everything, Wally."

"Please, Mr. Oglethrope." Chin trembling, Lynn stood. "Please. Wally's sorry."

"Sit down, Lynn." Oglethrope did not raise his voice.

"Can I go now?"

"By Tiwaz, sit down."

Lynn did not obey, stepped away from the table. She wore a pale pink shirt-dress with a wide skirt and a button-down collar. She rushed from the dining room, her hands over her face.

Oglethrope pointed at him. "If there's anything wrong with that girl, Dunford, I hold you responsible."

"Me?" He put the note in his pocket, hoping Oglethrope too mad to see him do it.

"You, Dunford. Just watch yourself."

He nodded, deciding not to answer. The longer he talked to Oglethrope, the longer it would take him to reach a place where he could read Lynn's note. He swallowed a few mouthfuls of pork, drank some water, and excused himself from the table. "I'll see you later, Wally."

"I had him moved, Dunford."

"Good evening, Mr. Oglethrope."

He headed for the cabin, pausing in an empty passageway to read: "PLEASE HELP MEET ME IN YOUR CABIN LYNN." He refolded the stiff paper, hurried on, opened the door, switched on the light.

She lay naked in the shadows of Wally's bunk, smoking a cigaret, but not inhaling. The elastic of her underpants had etched red lines around her thighs. "Please help, Mr. Dunford."

He closed the door, then wondered if he should open it again. "What do you want me to do, Lynn?"

"Golly me, Mr. Dunford. Don't be silly."

26

"OKAY. IF YOU TALKING that way." Only Friday morning would prove Hondo wrong. He slid his key into the lock. "You hungry?"

Hondo shook his head. "I'm going home." He lived in the nine-hundred block, a short walk.

"Okay." Carlyle wanted to say something, but did not know what. "Later. I'll see you."

Hondo managed a shrug, a smile. "Fair's fair, Carlyle."

The small yard's picket fence changed from gray to white as they stood and talked. In an hour, the sun would come up over the low brick rows of houses to start melting the snow. Carlyle watched Hondo away a half block, then stepped inside.

Mance, his brother, already dressed, knelt on the floor of his room, praying. They nodded, but did not speak. Just as Carlyle closed himself into his room, his mother's alarm rang, a second, no more. His father grunted.

He undressed, got into bed, tried to lie on his stomach, but his face was too sore wither cold. They water was getting hotter.

"You woo and your sense of chillevry. Sour Lancealot! But

Flutterybye, you sayd, Glalma's my old gayrlfriend! We got a
go to get her. We haifa do some ting! Like troy to breadk in the
Poxmies parity. Get tressed up and even shined our shines and
counterfrittered anviltations. Idle work, Butor. Id'll wack. You
think I heaven sent my lashes into a Peckpiece porty before.
But I news what lines to expact. Wait a minute, beys, let mist
ring up and isk if they rasking a visit from you. Buttorfly gets
iround. And one lilting I learnd: Keep your part ties sepiarated
from your swinegar vines and play the fool in the muddle."

"But he so bettorful, Boat. Ease my man." They water was
up to Gleama's waist, bubbling on her hedges. "Crylyle-sugar,
could you get Chief Pugmichillo to tan down the steam?"

"You whore a stewpead bitch! Nor wander you neba can
nest him, babylone. Tame down the stem! What dew he do, ax
him? Exuse me, Chiff, but turndown the stamp, S.V. Pleas."

"Honestly, you folks we people puzzle us.

The cold! you call: More coal, Jack Chill!

And now she haunts to hit our heat.

Of course, our code your systems frizz;

Fro Mafrica you came in boat.

Of course, the heat your systems bile.

We burn your meat to catch your wile.

You folks sure peoplepuzzle us."

Chief Pogmy Chill is head; he shook.

But Mr. Charile still was wishing they was some way to get
them to tone down the firelite, damp them. His face felt raw.

It grew dark already, the streetlight shining into his open
front-room window.

He rose and went to the bathroom. Nobody had come home.
His parents stopped in Harlem on Tuesday evening. Mance
attended his meeting.

He pissed, flushed, and inspected himself in the mirror, his
swollen face, his rooster's hair. He could not reach Butterfly's

Salon before closing, and sitting in a chair for that long with a face that sore did not appeal to him.

Dressing, he combed his hair the best he could, and walked to Bronxwood Avenue for some barbecue. He returned home and ate in front of the television, a movie, a mystery, some news. The late movies started dumbly, so he left the house and went around to Blue's Bar, drank some scotch and played six songs on the jukebox. But Hondo did not drop in and the new barmaid would not talk, so he walked the blocks home, undressed again, and climbed into that same kettle of fry, crussible as a cramberry.

They water was crocking Gluema's spout. "We sure venjoy ouSelfs until dhis happend, Charcoal, travelng all over. In Pyres, we vstay at dEtrole, in Roam at dColorseam. Bugbeds n Rhumservice. What aTrip! DHay vmake me feel so muffiful! Just like dAirgent sayd. Futtyfour punds aPace, n dontworry aBat about dHot-wetter. Well, at least mMunions meltng, n I ntcomplainng, but Curelull, sugarabbit, do somethinthinkthing!"

"Just in Hel what expect you he can do, nigression? You must be under some very powerful stiff. You must hink your heir is changing so tomorrow won't seem like yessoredays. We don't give a dime; time isn't any matter to the menu. Yar the history we said all about you. Yawl that property you read all about it!"

EXAFRA! Labor Content to Buy Forayon Deculturazed Whale's Blabbet! Swang at the Sworemony. Dout it? Dot dit? dit? dit it it tt t t t t tixshirty, and he had long since quit the Boy Scouts. But he could not return to sleep. And the house filled with noise, the family washing, dressing, eating. He got up and joined them at breakfast.

"Look who getting up with the birds." His father chewed roasted corn flakes.

Carlyle smiled. "I got night-time talent."

"You should use it in the service of the race." His brother drank only coffee in the morning. The day before he had taken his twice-monthly clean-head haircut.

"Man, how you be so serious at seven in the morning?"

His mother looked worried. "Don't fight you two."

"We ain't fighting, Mama." They answered together, and looked at each other, puzzled.

"Why you get your hair cut so short? You look like a cueball."

"Ever seen a black cueball?"

Carlyle did not entirely trust Mance's organization, the Black Jesuits, but at least they kept his brother straight, and had taught him to run a business.

They all had to hurry on to work: Mance to deliver bundles for a Jesuit store, his mother to clean a house, his father to guard a bank, gunless.

He stayed in the house until midmorning, then walked up the quiet street to Bronxwood Avenue to talk to Norman, who fumed because someone had tried to pressure him to sell MUFF, a little magazine of girls for young men. "I don't sell junk. Not with so many kids coming in here."

He drank a cup of coffee at Norman's counter, then took the subway to Harlem, and, remembering his dream, put in number 684, then went on to Butterfly's Salon, the first man to take a chair that morning.

"Baby, what happened to your head?"

"It got wet."

"We'll have to start from scratch."

Carlyle shrugged, watched Butterfly dump powder into a mug, then told him to stop. "Cut it off." He had no good reason, a joke on Mance. "Let's start before scratch."

"But, baby, are you serious?" Butterfly wrung his hands.

"You're so beautiful now." He took up his clippers. Later, he used depilatory from a blue can.

Carlyle looked at himself. He recognized his eyes, but his face had become older and younger at the same time, Carlyle bald, Carlyle before hair, like the pictures his mother saved. He got back into the chair for a facial.

The second man in the Salon, a kid, a serviceman, had just returned from Asia, complete with a hard-packed duffelbag. They got talking, and it happened that the kid carried with him, at the moment, thirty pounds of allegedly high-quality smoking material.

"I slept with it, jim, and I kept my uniform very neat."

They ducked into the back and sampled it, looking at the sky, talking on about Asia. The kid had liked the people, though they lived a different kind of life.

Butterfly banked him, and he bought the whole bag, knowing where he could sell it. In his head, he listed at least thirty secret smokers, men mostly, met at various parties in the Village, who, after conversation, had asked him to meet their demands.

He made phone calls from a bar down the street, scheduling appointments, stopping at fifteen to call Hondo. "I can't make all the drops in one day. So meet me by Air Chance's place."

The proposition did not catch Hondo's interest.

Working alone, he would have to do fifteen today, and fifteen tomorrow. After moving the duffelbag downtown by taxi and into Air Chance's place ("Oh, Juan, look at your beautiful head! You spending the afternoon with me? I fly tonight."), he began his deliveries. He wore his work clothes now, a short leather coat he left for emergency changes with Butterfly, had broken down the duffelbag into little-brown-bagfuls of what passed as sandwiches and coffee.

He stopped delivery at five, after fifteen, lightly threatened Air Chance against tampering with the duffelbag, and returned to Harlem for dinner. Later, at the Grouse, Cooley told him he would buy the remaining fifteen pounds. "But move it to Brooklyn for me, will you?"

Carlyle borrowed a car and drove downtown, wondering why he had not mentioned Hondo to Cooley.

Air Chance had flown to Europe; her roommate, expecting him, asked if he wanted to stay for a sandwich.

"No, baby, not now, but I'll be right back."

He returned straight to Harlem from Brooklyn, waited in the Grouse. By closing time, Hondo had not appeared, so he took a taxi home, hid his money, and went to bed.

"Too bad we kant order a caveyair with the alleycart. Art's? O din't you just love his prosiddick design, and those personelized cages with the foolusall-pattern? Whammerful, woterful, waterball we had! We can't white for simmer to finish til Thief Tschill says we can attack another two wreeks vancwation."

Dhay was already eatng. Him was the plotter in the table of the moddle.

"Pass a slice of peas of buff, Vili? Anybady want the Thaibone? Juno, I never believed genous could taste so kneet. I think we should pause a raisolution to atest to the effect that Cook Hinchill dide a reil good jab."

Day dicker doom:

"Tortle, nt-you wonder why Mr. Charcarl lieng like dhat dWay he have thave it?"

"Show o do, Rapit. Come on up out o'dPlater, Mr. Charleyle! Dhis dreamatic Epic-ode vfinishd almost."

"Pereodin me, jointlemen, but if you don't mind, wee'd like to see your rentrance cards. We know about these threed here, but you tude seem a shadowwhirlier set of wranglers. You do carry some fum of fidentificaution about you, don't you?"

"No, Mr. Hatchillmein. No. We vntcurry no imvitations. Sit up, Mr. Chacarl. Gater up yBones n Tings n we llready tmuvaut. No, Mr. Chencill, we vntget no Invitizements, just aDoom fo yTicker, aStick fo yFigure, aStone fo yImurge, doomdoom fo yBottom, tickertick fo yTope, toptop fo yTapper, boom-boom fo yBama, ticker doom tickticker, ticker tomb tickticker, bickerdoom tickertick, tititick dumaduma, tictitick bubbah-rhubbah, tatatow! Tow, titaw!

"Doomdoom   doomdoom   doomdoom   doomdoom, abcdeeef-ghhijklmnooooopqrrsttuuvwxyz, d-d t t d-d d-d d a a a a-a, kiki kikiki w-w-w ww wi-wi-wi wikik! Bbbbb b b brow! ow! run! F!F!F! aaaa a-a-a kssss, juju jujuju mmmmp z.O.o. vuvua daDa Dada dadhat dagdad lulu dalulu ae! zizzizi zeee, dhadow aa-daw awda alawd awdit oriold Dogone!"

"Dhey takeng care aBusiness!" Carlyle opened his eyes, sat up, smiled. "And did you see me duking in there?" He shook his head, looked at the clock: three-thirty; he had returned to his normal schedule.

In the bathroom, he surprised himself with his shaven head. He would have to get the clothes to go with it.

Left-over stew waited in the refrigerator; he warmed it in a frying pan. He would have grits, bacon and eggs for dinner, before he returned to bed.

The phone rang just as he sat down over his steaming plate.

"That you, Carlyle?"

"Yes, Mrs. Johnson. How you doing?"

"Well, a little better. Is Warren there?"

"Sorry, Mrs. Johnson."

She started to cry, and he asked her why.

"Warren said he gone to California today."

"Dhey takeng care aBusiness!"

27

"Now, DON'T YOU BE SILLY." He eased his hands into the pockets of his suit-coat, attempting to make himself appear more fatherly. "Whatever bothers you, well, you'll forget it tomorrow when the ship docks."

"Think so, Mr. Dunford?"

He had not averted his eyes—inspected her body, saw it clearly—collarbones, wrist-joints, blemish and hair. "I'm sure of it, Lynn."

"Don't you know what's bothering me, Mr. Dunford?" She sat up, dropped her cigaret into a silver bowl beside the bunk.

He shrugged. "Well, maybe I don't know exactly, but . . ."

She crossed her legs Indian-style, her elbows on her knees, her chin on her fists, as if listening to a story told at a campfire.

He talked: "But what I'm trying to say is that whatever it is that troubles you—understand?—it'll pass."

"Huh?" She scratched the bridge of her little nose with a snub-nailed index finger. "Come on, Mr. Dunford, first touch me all over with your big warm hands."

He took his hands from his pockets, grabbed the doorknob behind him. "Listen, Lynn, you don't really want to do this."

"You take a lot for granted, Mr. Dunford." Her voice rose higher, stayed flat. "Just because you're older than me doesn't mean you can tell me what I want to do."

"All right." He sighed. "I'm just trying to tell you that . . ." He thought, dared to speak honestly. "Sexual intercourse with me won't solve your problem, Lynn."

"Golly me, Mr. Dunford. Don't make me beg."

He leaned toward her, held the doorknob tightly. "Excuse me?"

"It's not right. Every time I meet one of you fellows you always make me beg."

"Beg?" One of who? "For what?"

"To golly me." She spread her arms, displaying her breasts. "Come on. I'm only fourteen years old."

"Fourteen years old?" She looked at least five years older.

"Did you read my file, Mr. Dunford?" She shrugged. "But my true age is seventeen years old."

"Lynn, wait a minute." He held up his hand, reminded himself he could trust his ears. "Look. Why don't you get dressed, and if you want, we can go to the lounge—"

"You can't golly me in the lounge." She looked puzzled, then smiled. "That would be real funny."

"But I'm not going to . . . golly you." He used her idiom, inspected her pale outline against the dark blankets. He wished Wendy lay there, scolded himself. "All right?"

"It's just not right! I know it's only an assignment, but it's not right for you to go out of your way to be mean. All the TYettes said you fellows acted very nice about going golly, but every time I . . ." She paused, looked at him. "Hey, Mr. Dunford, you're not Family Center-north, are you?"

He shook his head, trying to keep up.

"Some TYettes warned me about Family Center-north, said they'd kidnap you, but they said the Family West-northwest talked tough, and demanded respect, but could get real sweet, and you know, and that Family Center fellows liked to go golly when they weren't working, because everybody knows business comes first with the Family." Her silver eyes glazed to mercury. "Though Mary-Joan Dinley even lived with a Family Center agent when she was assigned to the Cameroons. Until the authorities found out." She shook her head. "But she went too far, having a baby and all. But I'm assigned to you so take off your clothes."

He still did not understand, but her mention of Africa interested him. Hoping she would continue to talk, he began to unbutton his shirt. Then he realized he still wore his suit-coat, took it off and hung it on the doorknob, continued with his buttons. Besides, she no longer seemed the troubled teenager, and after Wendy, quite suddenly, he felt mean. "You're making a mistake, Lynn."

"You must be new, Mr. Dunford. Didn't any Family tell you about the TYettes?"

"I don't think so." He pulled out his shirttail.

"They should've. All we do is go sneakers and golly." She reflected. "I was fourteen when Daddy signed me up, and I don't remember doing anything at all. But after Basic, I was just like everybody. Hurry up, Mr. Dunford. Wally'll come in fifteen minutes."

He stopped unbuckling his belt. "Fifteen minutes?"

"I go very fast."

"Where's Wally now?" And how did she know?

"Over in the office with Mr. Oglethrope. We might even have time for two."

He chanced one more question. "With the slaves?"

Her silver eyes snapped shiny. "With the cargo. Ya. You recording, Mr. Dunford?"

"No, Lynn."

"Because Mr. Oglethrope goes real berserk if I get recorded." She shook her head. "You and Whitman really have him flummoxed. We were told it was only her, and maybe a backstop. Now he doesn't know how many . . . Please hurry, Mr. Dunford."

He put his right arm back into his shirt. "Listen, Lynn, wait here a minute." She had decoyed him.

"Where're you going?"

"I have to go . . . to the infirmary."

"Don't worry, Mr. Dunford. After Mary-Joan, the authorities called us back for adjustments." She patted the bunk. "Honest, Mr. Dunford, in three years both on the north and south Atlantic run—"

He opened the door, stepped out. "I'll be right back." He ran.

"Stop, Mr. Dunford!" Lynn followed him into the hallway. He glanced back, saw the pistol's hole between her breasts, made the corner, hoping he could find the slaves again, and save Wendy.

One level up, he stopped running, reasoning that Lynn would have to dress. Besides, he did not exactly know the way. The first time, he and Wally had happened onto the slaves, or Wally had led him. And Wendy had guided the second time.

He tried to follow Wendy's way, finding the narrow spiral stair they had reached from the deck. But why take her way? Perhaps the Family also dealt in slaves. She had not hesitated to call him nigger. Why even want to save her? Because he knew her.

Halfway down, he realized a door waited at the bottom, then a foyer, off the passageway. He stopped and tried to think of a plan. After a few moments he gave up. He did not know enough to plan, would have to walk into the passageway, and improvise.

In the foyer, he began to hear voices, two men arguing behind a closed door. He stepped out into the passageway. The voices grew louder, Oglethrope and Wally. He tiptoed to the door of the cabin where he and Wendy had found the slave manifest.

"You're all wet, Mr. Oglethrope."

"I been at this longer than you, kid."

"I'm telling you, if we do it your way, it'll jam. The TYO480 won't accept it. Honest, Mr. Oglethrope, this is something new."

"Back off, Wally. I've done these things since the war, and I know how to make them short and brief. You think I'm not acquainted with the agent who reviews our work? We know how we operate; we got an understanding."

"This is a new procedure. They don't want just plain cancels. They want us to report in detail."

"That's the stupidest thing I ever heard, Wally. We fill in the blanks and go back to work."

"Well, all right, Mr. Oglethrope. I can't dispute my superior, but I think it's only fair to say I'm planning to submit my own report."

"You got your channels, and I got mine. But don't take credit for my cancel."

Their argument finished, Oglethrope grunted and Wally whistled. Chig left the door and crossed the hall. Perhaps he would find Wendy with the slaves. He twisted the knob to the padded room.

"Ready for some exercise, Mr. Dunford?" Lynn had crept up behind him on her pink sneakers. She had dressed herself in blue trousers with sewn-in creases and a white T-shirt, TIWAZ YOUTH ORGANIZATION misshapen across her breasts. "What muscles you want to start with?"

He looked for her pistol, did not find it. "You have a key?" He made a joke, hoping he would not have to hurt her.

"Sure, Mr. Dunford." She reached into her back pocket, pulled out her key, bent to the lock, and opened the door.

A punching bag hung from the pink wall; a leather exercise-horse waited welded to the padded floor. Gloves curled in the corner, a medicine ball not far away.

Lynn closed the door behind them. "We have to talk fast, Mr. Dunford. Were you kidding in the cabin?"

He had not yet recovered from the room, nodded.

"Yes?" She whispered. "Don't be mean now, Mr. Dunford."

Every trace of the Africans had disappeared.

She put her square little hand on his arm. "I'm real sorry you lost this game, Mr. Dunford. Did you know her well?" From her pocket, she produced a stub of pencil, went to a pad of paper hanging on a chain near the parallel bars. "I would never get a feeling for Wally. When he got cancelled, I'd be sad."

He did not move. "Wh . . . Whitman's cancelled?"

"Sure, Mr. Dunford. So I'm giving you my address in New York in case you change your mind." She tore off a sheet of paper, then sprawled on the padded floor, her knees bent, her feet wagging, her tongue clamped between her lips, and began to write. "Were you in love, Mr. Dunford?"

"Yes." Again, he had taken too long.

"That's nice. Maybe I'll fall in love one day, but never inside TYO. And Family fellows are out of the question." She made a face. "They showed us movies of Mary-Joan Dinley."

He remembered the name, guessed. "She lived with an African?"

"I guess so. He was Family Center. You're Family West-northwest, aren't you?"

He nodded, afraid to speak.

"What Family was she, Mr. Dunford?" She finished writing, jumped to her feet, waving the paper at him. "I told Mr. Oglethrope she was Family Center-north, but—"

"Wendy's Family?" Wow.

She shook her head. "You mean you didn't know either? This was really some game." She smiled sweetly, lowered her silver eyes. "It's the most interesting since I joined."

"So you lost this game, Dunford." Oglethrope stood just inside the now open door. "Next go, maybe you'll get the breaks. But not against this TYO Team." He slapped his stomach. "For a while, your offensive had me fooled. I was looking at another colored girl." He winked his seeing eye. "A ginger-cake. Where'd Whitman say she was from?"

"Virginia." He could not help smiling: Wendy came from Virginia, had worked for the Family, had died. He had heard it all in the nigger, but had not seen her through her skin. "Family West-northwest."

Chig turned to Lynn, who still held her address in her hand. "You finished with that, Lynn?"

"Finished, Mr. Dunford." She looked at Oglethrope, crumpled the directions in her fist. "Maybe next time."

"Right! This game is over." Oglethrope cleared his throat. "Dunford, I know you're new in the game, and maybe it'll surprise you that through the years some customs, you might call them, have grown up between TYO and you boys. You might wonder why we didn't cancel you. Simple. We transferred the cargo, so why spill oil we don't have to?" He hesitated. "Anyway, after we take the prize we usually offer you boys a beer, you know, and we all toast the cancelled. So I'm hoping you'll join us."

He looked at the ex-athlete, then the girl. They outnumbered him. "Thank you, Mr. Oglethrope, but not tonight. I couldn't possibly." He shook his head. "No."

28

"HE SAID WHAT?" He still could not believe it. "When he tell you this?"

Mrs. Johnson coughed, a squack on the wire. "Today he said he leaving on the evening plane."

"Stupid motherfucker."

"What?" He did not repeat himself. "It's you, Carlyle Bedlow, you and your fast mouth!"

He hung up on her, wondering how her round brown face had looked. For a moment at least, he had made her forget worry.

So Hondo had decided to give his body to the Devil, so the Devil could sell it back. For his mother's thousand? Probably not. But perhaps the Devil knew how much Cooley Johnson earned each week, knew of Cooley's connection to Bumper Henderson, who might pay not to get squeezed. Hondo might have a value of as much as fifty thousand dollars to somebody.

"Me."

Thinking of his clean head, he chose his clothes, light gray-green wool pants, a sky-blue turtleneck sweater, rubber-soled walking shoes for moving quickly, then put on his camel's-hairs and tied the buckleless belt. He would need a driver, a man who did not look suspicious. He called Butterfly.

"But the Salon's steaming with business, customers waiting. There's not one chair vacant."

"How long it take you to make thirteen thousand dollars?"

"Baby, how you talk!"

They agreed to meet at the Salon. By the time Carlyle arrived, Butterfly would have searched through his old copies of The Citizen to find the ad that had hooked Hondo. The Devil probably ran a loan company as a front for kidnap. He would investigate anybody who came in, and if he found hidden money in a background, would launch the Devil game. Hondo's mother, Carlyle realized, always got sick, always got well, always felt pain somewhere, but always worked. Like his own mother.

He pulled the spread over his unmade bed, went out into the kitchen and put his uneaten plate into the refrigerator.

He still did not believe in Hondo's Devil, but on his way out of his home, he broke off a clove of his mother's garlic, buried it in his pocket.

The taxi ride took thirty minutes; he sat back on the hard plastic seat and closed his eyes, but did not sleep.

"I found it." Butterfly waited at the door, handed him a neatly clipped advertisement, the size of a matchbox. "See? We loan to anybody."

He memorized the address. "Come on, man."

They good-byed Butterfly's barbers, who stopped their scissors to bat their eyes, then walked out into the street. "You're so grim and beautiful, baby."

He nodded. "You carrying a gun?"

"Sorry. It's at my apartment. We could go there."

"We running too late." The streets shone slick with melting snow.

"You're terrible."

Butterfly's car gleamed lemon-yellow in the early darkness, its windshield bright with sky. They opened the doors, climbed into the black leather coach.

"You know where we going, Butterfly?"

"Yes, baby." He whirled the wheel, steering them out into traffic. "But why?"

"Somebody trying to kidnap my man Hondo."

"So he's my rival."

"Your rival, man, be women."

Butterfly stopped for a red light. "Only men really understand the problems of men."

"A woman don't got to understand. She just got to listen real good."

"Who listens better than me?"

"Probably nobody, man."

They crossed two avenues. Butterfly beat the light of a third before he spoke again. "Then aren't you interested?"

Carlyle shook his head. "Not until women stop."

Butterfly sighed. "And they so many of them too."

"Millions, man." He and Butterfly had to come to an agreement before going into battle. "But, you see, it's my duty."

Butterfly glanced at him, did not comment.

He took a deep breath. "Man, all I hear all the time, there be more women than men, women walking around looking for men, and they not that many men. So anytime women come your way, you got to do them, understand what I mean? All these women wandering around looking for men, if you don't do them, they'll see they doing all right by themselves. Then, they'll stop looking for men, and settle down, seven and eight to a room, living all in the cities. Then, man, they'll see they in the majority and vote themselves into power. And when that happen, where will you be at?"

Butterfly poked out his lips. "Well, what can I do?"

"Tie them down, man. Knock them up and give them something to think about. You dig it? Make men, man."

"But, baby, I already did that."

Carlyle laughed. "Then you understand what I'm talking about." He stared at Butterfly. "Right?"

Butterfly waited to answer. "I hate to lose you."

He placed his hand on Butterfly's arm. "You ain't lost me, baby. You just found me. We can be friends." He paused until Butterfly had turned to look at him. "Now ain't that some simple shit!"

Butterfly began to laugh, offered his right hand for a slap, then made a left into the Devil's street. Carlyle watched the numbers, searched the doorways of dark warehouses, until straight ahead, he found the limousine, brake-lights aglare, waiting at the corner for the signal to change. He pointed. "Move up, Butterfly."

Without a lurch, Butterfly gave them speed, carried them close enough to see the out-of-state license: WC-5, rusted symbols on a plate of dark-red, and above it, through the oval window, the back of Hondo's head. "They got him."

Butterfly sucked his tongue. "What do we do now?"

"We follow."

The limousine took a right, going south, stopped at the corner of the street, went right again, passing bars: B.Q.'s, Hare's Lair, The Brown Turtle, The Oasis Palm, Jesse B.'s Joyce Club, Brown's, Mr. Mitey's Blessed Diner, Melvin's Jazzmatazz Gallery, Smokey's Smoother Room, Rinehart's Restaurant, T.M.'s

Dream Room, Sonny R's Boom Bar, The Johnson Jones Jail House, all of them open, flashing, and filling up—until a light caught them at the clock by the diamond store.

They turned north on the Avenue; they would pass the Grouse. "Pull up on the right of them."

Butterfly swung out, moved up, inches away. Ma Buster drove, the chauffer's cap mashed over her curls. The Devil sat in the rear, directly behind her. Hondo sagged in the backseat's center, his neck and shirt-front ablaze with points of light. "When we reach in front of the Grouse, smash them."

"Thirteen thousand dollars, Carlyle?"

"If you wreck the car, man."

"You're sweet." Butterfly squealed, swerved to his right for an angle, then guided his lemon fender, crunching low and hollow, into the limousine's front door. Ma Buster opened her mouth, but nothing came through the glass. Butterfly floored the pedal now, bulldozed the limousine sideways into the stone divider running down the middle of the Avenue. The cars stopped.

Carlyle climbed out slowly, shouting: "Devil, you a menace!"

On the sidewalk in front of the Grouse, two boys in leather coats, sunglasses, and an old lady with a brown paper shopping bag halted, interested.

"Get out that car! Let me teach you something!"

Ma Buster stared, her cap crooked on her head, trapped. The back compartment seemed empty until Hondo rose from the floor, blinking, opened the door, and tumbled out onto the black asphalt. Around his neck, he wore a bejewelled dog's collar, the leash swinging free.

The Devil appeared, stepped down, in a dark suit, pink shirt with big cuff-links, dark tie, polished, pointed black shoes. His face had not changed. "What is this?"

"Never mind talk. Get ready to go for your gun!" Carlyle

yelled, looking back at the sidewalk, where a crowd of people gathered, a man with a metal loaf-shaped lunchbox, another man rolling a newspaper, two short ladies in short wool coats. The boys in leather had begun an inspection of the point of impact. "You see that mother fender curl man?"

"Why did you destroy our car?" The Devil stepped closer, eyes narrowed, his breath colder than the air. "Tell us your name."

"No." Carlyle paused, thought, then smiled. "You don't know my name?"

"Now just a minute, young man."

"Just a minute, your mama."

Hondo had managed to sit now.

"Get on your feet, Mr. Johnson!" Carlyle made his voice stern. "Your master speaks to you!"

"Yes, sir." Hondo shook his head, put his hands on the asphalt, and struggled to stand. He recognized Carlyle—who winked, then smiled at the Devil.

"I don't like nobody running my game. You understand?" He turned away, addressed the crowd on the sidewalk. "You know what he just said? That he's the Devil."

"He do?"

Carlyle whispered to the Devil. "There can be only one Devil. You or me. You can't have it both ways." He turned his back, hollered at the crowd. "Who saw what this devil did?"

A giant black man in a leather cap stepped forward. "I seen it, bubbah, and it was him!"

They all stepped forward then, pressed in around the two cars. "I seen it too men came right out of where he did like that time we went over to Tennessee it come up here in his big black lemon car!"

The Grouse had emptied, ten or fifteen men he knew standing up on the Avenue divider, toasting him with their drinks.

Butterfly rested his head on the steering wheel, sobbing for his beautiful machine. "But look, it's junk now." Several of his gentlemen friends from the Grouse had filled the seats, consoling him.

The streetlight came on. "What I always heard right there the most accidents happen when I seen it went all the way over out his chauffer laid there behind the wheel out some drinks, Jim!"

Carlyle threw the Devil a shrug, patted the lump in his pocket. "If the Devil's me, you'll never make it. And if he's you, you still might not make it."

"Listen, him and Everett Cooper be riding along one night when Coop have his coupe with the leathertop of the grade, they saw a great big grizzly bear standing in the tunnel as much as you please, man, but move out the way! I can't see nothing neither nigger get so upset his whole chassis slipped all over every which place. But it was him."

The Devil frowned, bit his upper lip, nodded, then climbed back into the limousine. He pulled the door behind him, and pressed down the button on the windowsill. Ma Buster swiveled in the driver's seat, smiled at her passenger. Then the inside of the limousine burst bright with fire, burning.

"Jump back! That car gone in and take my jacket, Jackson. I don't need it. This mama hotter than a mammyjammy. Stand back, baby, or you'll get your boobies hatching! Get that kid out the night come these two cars here up the Avenue and me be peeping from behind the park, when for no reason, that black one go after the ambulance, man, but I think them people trapped. I didn't see the beginning, but from the ending what I think happened that a young married couple on they honeymooning got lost. I wondered why that devil went in his car, but couldn't get it started. Then they got a flat. The cat fixed the tire before they could get moving again, the motor exploded.

So they had to walk up that hill to this castle. And it was cold, rainy and knocked. The door open and sheee, what a beautiful woman with long black hair playing that girl everybody says passed in a nightgown, fine as fantabulous!"

"Carlyle, don't think I don't appreciate what you did." Hondo turned from the blaze, his face too serious above the jewel-studded dog's collar. "But if you bringing sickness back in my mama's life, I'll never forgive you, Ras."

"Don't worry, man." Even with his camel's-hairs and the fire, he felt chilly. "That woman'll live forever."

29

"Just a second, bud. I don't think I understand. You act like you believe I didn't like her." Oglethrope nodded his head, once. "But I did. I watched her offensive, and at the end, of course, we took the prize." He stopped, grinned. "Yes, sir, boy!"

Chig did not want to hear about the prize, not quite yet. He raised his wrist, checked the time, almost nine. "No thanks. I want to get some sleep." He paused, added for protection, "This was my first game."

"Sure, Dunford." He turned on Lynn. "You see how these boys play for keeps? That's the way you have to be if you want to expect to win."

"But, Mr. Oglethrope, you assigned me to go—"

"Good night, everybody." Chig hurried, calmly, to the door.

"I assigned you a mousetrap, Lynn. But you got to vary your offensive. You don't golly every time you get ass—"

Chig stepped out of the padded room, into the passageway. The door to the cabin stood open. Inside, Wally sat at the desk, writing. Chig did not stop.

Back in his cabin, he sat on Wally's bunk, shook his head.

He tried to picture Wendy's parents, light-skinned Virginians of African descent, passing perhaps. But probably not; more than likely, they just lived ordinary light-skinned lives. His own parents had acquaintance with at least three such couples. Chig had met their children at parties.

He undressed, put on his pajamas, bent over the little wash-basin to brush his teeth. He had liked Wendy's smile, her dimple, a mole on her chin. He wished he had met her before he left for Europe the first time, but sensed that neither of them would have liked the other.

"Wow." He tapped his toothbrush against the basin, replaced it in its glass tube, readied himself for the climb into bed, and climbed, but could not sleep, rolled from side to side in the narrow bunk, fearing that each passing step brought Oglethrope to his cabin, sweating in the tight space, pulling down the legs of his pajamas, flattening the buttons against his chest, pushing back the blanket, then the sheet, punching his pillow, for hours, and hours, and hours.

He gave up at seven in the morning, dressed and tottered to the dining room to breakfast with poached eggs on wet toast, coffee. Then he went on deck.

The sky domed blue, cloudless, high; the sun rose over the stern of the ship. He walked toward the bow, thinking about the Africans and the ways they might have gotten off the ship. And Wendy. Stopping at the rail, he leaned over to look for a cargo door in the ship's hull, found only fields of gray rivets, neatly joined slabs of steel.

He closed his eyes, saw the rivets' shadows in bright colors, and wondered whether his eyes, and not his ears, had spoiled; his jest did not cheer him.

He returned to his cabin, set his watch, but did not change clothes, and climbed into his bunk, but again could not sleep. Instead he built Wendy's face in his mind, having difficulty coloring her. She always turned out too ashen, unhealthy, untanned.

He abandoned her face for her voice, tried to recall having heard a trace of the nigger at another time in the years he had known her. But the nigger had stayed well hidden. Still, he felt he should have known. She had always known, the inside knowing what the world believed the outside to represent. He should have known too, at their first meeting. He had never missed before. But then, he realized that as a professional, Wendy had trained to make him miss.

He sat up, dangled his legs over the edge, then swung down to the floor. He laughed as he tucked in his shirt, counting the hours he had wasted trying to sleep, then climbed the stairs to the crowded decks, old women in black, old men in gray, lining the railings for a look at the city, already within the range of sight: tall hills of buildings on black water, haloed by yellow smoke.

He watched it loom closer, then turned, running in his mind, but walking into the lounge. He did not feel ready for that yet.

Sucking some kind of cherry-colored liquid through a straw, Lynn sat in the curved corner seat where he and Wendy had met the afternoon before. He set himself to flee, and watched her. She wore a dark-blue travelling dress, buttoned to the throat, red barrettes in her hair. She did almost look fourteen, a girl in an advertisement for training-brassieres. But what she knew would fill books. And she had seemed really to want him to know her address. He made himself approach her. "Hello, Lynn."

"Mr. Dunford?" She smiled up at him, whispered, "I tried to get down to your cabin last night, but . . ." She sucked on her drink.

"I understand." He slid in beside her. "But, Lynn?" He hesitated. "Where do you stay in New York?"

"Golly, Mr. Dunford, I'm sure glad!" She leaned closer, the

straw still between her lips. "Can you remember? In Westchester, you know the area code, Richland 850—"

"I hope I can sit down, sugar, because this Harriet is surely pooped."

He looked up; she wore brown-rimmed glasses like cat's eyes. "Sure, Harriet did you say?" The table would not allow him to stand. "Have a seat."

She smiled, thanked him, bounced into a chair on the outside of the curved table. "You been on board this whole trip and I didn't see you?" She seemed made of gingerbread.

He nodded, wondering what Lynn thought. "Lynn, this is Harriet."

"Hi, Harriet." She turned her head slowly, stared at him. In her eyes, he saw fear.

Harriet leaned forward, peered through her glasses. "How long you been in Europe, dear?"

"Huh?" A smile fluttered across her lips. "Well, like my Mom says, three's a crowd, Mr. Dunford. And I have to find Wally." She wiggled her nose, then slid around to the end of the seat. "He's my boyfriend, Harriet. Bye-bye, Mr. Dunford."

"I'll call you, Lynn." He gazed at her sturdy legs, her loafered feet, as she walked to the door. He hoped he remembered the number correctly.

"Now that she's gone, sugar, tell me your name too."

He told her Charles, but that most people called him Chig.

"Charles." She nodded, her head covered with brown curls the size of half-dollars. "Charles. Chig. Charles, I could never begin to tell you how tired this sister is. Nothing but travel for a whole month. The first week I was on a tour, but then I didn't go with them people anymore, just walked around looking. I bought some beautiful shoes in Rome, thinking they'd be nice for my job, but sugar, I walked those shoes to death." She stared at him, brown eyes magnified. "What did you do?"

He considered the question impolite. "I travelled around."

She cleared her throat. "I'm a writer."

He did not comment.

She wore a red shirt, black crepe slacks. "I mean I cover society news and human interest for The Citizen. It's Harlem's only daily newspaper."

"I remember seeing it."

"You lived in Harlem?"

"All my life until I left. Over by the drive. My folks still live there." He decided he had nothing more to say to her, and told her he wanted to go to his cabin. "I still have to pack."

"I hope you don't mind my coming with you, sugar. I'll help."

He could not stop her returning with him to his cabin, or from pushing him away from his own bag, or packing for him. He thanked her, confessing he felt tired. She took him and his bag to her cabin, gave him a drink from a bottle of brandy, bought in Europe, which she had planned to save for the editor of The Citizen. He watched her pack her bright clothes into one suitcase, then finished his brandy.

They carried their things up on deck, more crowded still, the buildings over them now, and witnessed the ship docking, ropes and streamers linking ship to shore.

Harriet continued to talk, detailing for him her month in Europe. "Sugar, those people are poor!"

They quit the ship, did not wait for a porter, stepped unassisted from gangplank to asphalt pier, commenting that they continued to feel the sway of the ship. "How long will it last, sugar? I feel drunk. And I don't like feeling drunk since I drank so much in Paris. I have a girlfriend living there, who used to model natural wigs, living with a painter from Yugoslavia it turned out—"

"Is your bag unlocked?" He had just remembered Customs.

"I think so." She cocked an eye at him. "And yours?"

He nodded. "I never carry anything they want. I don't smoke."

"You trying to tell me something, Charles?" She had a way of jiggling when she walked, even carrying a heavy suitcase.

They joined the Customs line. Ahead of them, in a chained-off enclosure, uniformed inspectors ran their hands along trunk-linings, under shirts—squeezed ties, patted panties, opened cases, valises, and purses, searching.

"Like what?" He put down his bag, reached for his passport. He hoped the inspectors would not find his picture too dated.

Harriet's passport shone dull-green and new. "Like matchboxes."

"I don't usually carry matches."

"I bet you don't. Give the man your thing, your passport, sugar."

He had shuffled forward, guiding his bag with his foot, had reached the head of the line with his back to the inspector, behind him in a mesh-cage. He turned, displayed his passport, his eyes on the inspector's metal buttons, all dented and crushed. "Looks real at a distance, bud, but let me see it close up."

The inspector reached out, seized his passport, thumbed it. "Feels good too." He took Harriet's passport, slapped the two together, and folded his hands around them. "You folks related?"

"No, sir." He tried to stand at attention, did not want to fidget. "We met on the ship."

"Fast work, Dunford. Nice." He stamped their passports, handed them back. "Welcome home." He winked his left eye, watched them with his right, then stood up in the cage and shouted to an inspector near the door. "Hey, Burison, let these folks in!"

They crossed the enclosure, brushed by Burison's belly as

they passed through the door he held for them, carried their bags the length of the covered pier to the cobblestone street, and reaching the corner, rested.

"They always so nice, Charles?" She looked at him as if she idolized him. "Or was it just you?"

"That's usual." He wondered how long it would take her to realize she did not interest him, no matter how attractive she appeared. "For everybody."

"He certainly acted like he knew you."

"He doesn't." The idea surprised him.

They had to wait twenty minutes, feeling the city summer in the buildings like steam in radiators, had to wave their arms forty times, but finally a taxi stopped. The driver wanted to go to Harlem anyway, to eat. "So you two just come back from the far side of the big water."

"That's right, sugar." Harriet sat on the edge of the seat, blinking at the city from behind her glasses.

The taxi was going to crash.

"Honeymoon?" The driver looked at them in his mirror, a large shiny dark-brown nose over a mustache, two dark eyes under a narrow brim. "Or funnymoon? I wouldn't tell."

Harriet sucked her tongue. "Well, thank you."

"You welcomed, baby." He nodded in the mirror, gassed the motor, climbing the ramp onto the drive going up the west side of the island. "Have fun? I know you did. I always cruise where the ships docking. Always one or two cousins coming in. So I know."

Before they crashed, he would have to tell the driver to leave the drive and let them out.

"You two young people starting out quiet. I like that." He shook his head. "Now me and Mama be another story."

He would have to tell the driver to stop right there on the drive, and let them out, before they crashed. He did not want to die yet. He had just begun to realize what had happened, what they had come through. He started to shake, hoping Harriet and the driver did not see.

"What's the matter, sugar?" Harriet leaned toward him. She smelled spicey, like cloves. "You're shaking."

"Yes." He tried to stop himself. "I know."

"What's wrong, bubbah?" The driver's eyes filled the mirror. "Don't tell me you people hot. Oh, shit!"

"Charles, what's the trouble? Oh goodness, what's his other name? Chig?"

He sat up, still shaking. "I'm tired." Wendy had pronounced Chig just that way, holding the short vowel long, soft on the final consonant, the trace. "I'm just tired, man, am I tired." He took a deep breath, quaking, then felt trouble pass. "Listen. Do you know a nice café?"

"Sure, bubbah. Want some liquor?"

He had imagined himself in Europe, realized again he was in New York. "In a nice place."

"The nicest!" The driver sped, knowing his destination, happy to go there. He wove the lanes, gliding, braking, the taxi a smooth-moving package of rattles, until he left the drive and hit the stretch passing Soldier's Tomb. He came to a full stop, looked both ways, cursing the hidden police, and made his turn into Harlem.

"Dig, the place I'm taking you have a history. Not just one of your little monthly opening with a cocktail-sip bars that never caught on, and had its windows waxed over in six months. You follow music? Then, man, you in for the thrill of your life, because this bar's owner be none other than the Golden One himself, Jack O'Gee."

"I've been there." Harriet puckered her lips. "And I don't mind telling you—"

"You right, sister. Listen, you be sitting in the Grouse and anybody might happen to come in. All kinds of distinguished ladies and gentlemen, congressmen, beauty-parlor queens, number-runners, judges, musicians, movie stars, preachers, visiting taxi-fleet owners from Chattanooga, the manager of the ex-fly-weight-champion of the world, Skeeter Jimson, I met one night, Cripple Christopher on his wooden leg, Shorty Moreland the midget m.c. and just about any other bodies you could think of." He swung left around an avenue-divider, double-parked the taxi, and opened his door. "I'll just have me a little taste too."

They climbed out. The driver told them to leave their bags in the trunk; he would stop the meter, and if they bought the drinks, he would take them home after a while, for free.

On the three-step stairway leading down into Jack O'Gee's Golden Grouse Bar and Restaurant, Harriet grabbed his arm, whispered: "He still thinks we travelled together, Charles."

He held the door for her. "That's all right."

The Grouse had air-conditioning. ". . . as my body had been in at that time, if he ever try to pull some knife on me, man, and you buy the next do it whenever I get to drinking, I also get to thinking about we, Marky Electo, and Julius Chambernard, his brother Roger, and Norton Williams standing in that same bar bell or something, a bus-stop sign with a stone bottom on her Paul and Terry picked that mother over his head with one hand and pressed it five or ten times a day I be getting up and running to the bathroom last winter some or other time, I recall, staying home and the snow start falling by the window. Now I never been exactly what you'd call a Polar-bear, you understand, but that snow sure looked seven kinds of good to me. Because of what me and my man've just go through. Right, Juan?"

Juan had shaved his dark-brown head bald like some imitation movie star. He smiled, did not speak.

The driver had guided them to a table against the wall, ushered them inside to a long upholstered bench running the length of the room. He sat across from them, his hat on the table. "You see? The Grouse always—"

"—trying to tell you something about the time I sold my soul to the damn Devil, then took that soul right straight back again." The speaker leaned forward, a little mustache above a wide mouth in the middle of a round brown face. He sat at the next table, addressing someone beyond the man called Juan. "Not that I ever got convinced by his Devil stuff, even after he made me sign my name in blood. The man have some money for me. But Juan, he started to carry garlic around in his pocket!"

Juan nodded. Without hair, without a voice, he could have come from anywhere. Dark enough to pass for an African, his clothes had a South American flair.

"And we got some money. Devil had me put on this dog collar beat out of gold and covered with precious stones, and then, went away and forgot I was wearing it. We sold it to what they call a private collector for, now let me tell you, twenty—"

"Hondo be one of the fastest-mouthed cousins I ever heard." The driver smiled, one tooth glittering. "Every time I see him, he have a new story."

"You know him?" Harriet touched the driver's hand, a sister's touch. "To talk to?"

"Know him!" The driver seemed slightly insulted. "Why he come in here almost much as me."

Harriet leaned back, put her hand on his cheek. "Charles, you'll have to forgive me, sugar, but I want to do a little work."

"Yes. All right." He allowed himself to slide down on his spine, and relax. "Human interest for The Citizen. Go on, Harriet. I'll wait for you. No one's expecting me. I can stay out as long as I want."

30

LET HIM STRAY OUT long as he walk? Furever? Forgive him h'whatface Mustchaff? After all dRastas he vlash? After all dRastorations he vrob? Whymen, sooner later dhan never I llsee aNoose o some Thong sore h'sotty Neck, aGallowtine from San Francesicko separate hHad from hLag. He got aTerm tride out! Muvaut, men, n catch Hatch Chillmean!

Lylies n chartlemen, turn up yRears n getready dSet on go, showly, cause here, fo Sister Sinah over Vic's Bar, n dWogs n Gailys in Aimiddleville n Isleepo Centro (Gar she ya soon), Jaimmey n Mercy, Ruby Prosita n que linda; Luis (Itwaz all aDream) n Hazelle (she vshine so beautiful just up from lowest-norest) n Larry (when ll-he, Mary?), contrary Krissy n Keven d'original Manboy (six add plus z'eight tseven him now, true Irise?); t'dGib, sons, Sall n Everey, wi a'spacelle Ello tGeorge Pear; n sheetward ttoast Crispytina, Jaijikai's older Image liv-eng in Bannisterburg on dBanks o'dPatomoania wi Ham, gentle Journie, n aSprig o'Misheltwo; n call dCousins in Chattera-nooga t'dRamiophone, n dCoscions in Feelee t'dAuroaraset; till dNewfockses on Lastrala tbarn Burnett's Cheek n pat hBabys;

file aReporter o three on dLookout tsay Hello tFarmiliargent
Adolf Akima, bouyant n manng dSunraises in dCameraroons;
best wishes t'dHoneyable Gouverneur Simon n h'paint House!!
Foriver Hutson. A gail brown Hand fo dUncle in dBand.
ASymbol fo Steve. AKingdome fo Keeys. ASomba fo Beniny
comeng later in dShowndown at sinrest. A'freyr Hand fo Ernst
Aux Togo. ABang fo barrychestd Francis. Fo aTonde a'fine

*D'mudcap n wheelarious Escapeaids o'Rab n Turt, two
o'NewAfriquequerque's toughfast, ruefest Spaciel Constubulary
Texnosass Arangers.*

young Plunger, no matter dThs. A'all-Stone fo A Andar-san.
Moveng on tbestowe Bestoweshis on Treiver Stiffone, dPrin-
chief, from Ilbe Eleke n all dQuills n Brushs in Kingstoneton-
townships (brethr):

DMaker o'Babaslick Coils n Springs (in unconjoind Con-
junktion wi dGrist Shipnayer Loines) present:

D'mudcap n wheelarious Escapeaids o'Rab n Turt, two
o'New Afriquequerque's toughfast, ruefest Spaciel Constubulary Texnosass Arangers.

Eveready dhem? You bright. Wire course, flash Week o only lash Night, when d'all Professor vrecount fo you (n d'lessenng Pleasure o'ou'everfadey, interlokitng Odiounce) some o'd'ussential Acepix o'd'respectd Dheistory o'dhese travailng Bifriends, des gents C. Turtom (aAx) n S. Rabisam (aSnax), dTourtease n dHire (tmoccasin aSample), dDuelty (dhis dGuise o'Canflick) o'ou'comproviseng, collactivateng, constantual Consense.

Sosssspread dPoelms o'yHands on d'circulbar Tabletop n feel dBubbarhymble o'dBreathers o'a'free Airtime. Withdrawninwinwithin Chiarlyle Donelow, Buttlerbattler, n do a'expluraltory kultur Surch in what mightcall hSelf dIntomate-Posture, n findhat aMass o'Movengmumbleng vpile dPast on dOreillely-Pressent.

From d'firest Day, when Liverstone Chilney vvapowerize on dCongo Ribbah, dhen n on after dSale n dBought venreach Mr. Rocker Wheelchase, dVoice o'Af Ricco vpour C. Walker Tortumn n S. Rider Wappit dGrape o'dVine, makeng aCertan ouNaturesteem llcontinue tbake in d'collarest Port o'd'backest Lot o'd'fartest-out Scene o'dBallet o'Storm Macker, 1770 Whalesian Crushent, Strangleterre. (V-he know her? V-E nudjet her? O v-he tell him about her?) Doe batter what Nut you doeng, dVoice o'Yomamabubbah-calmng, calkng, comeng over dTabletin in Gribs n Graby, across d'big Fence from Mamouth t'Babouche, true dToot o'Been n Bird's airs, by Pongo Santa Chanoya, llrich ewe. You Tall King; me Take Kin. Me Tackng; you Lassong. Abong! Abang! Day dicker dome, Abeng!

In ou'last Epicode, dhen, Coats Turtical, h'subnosed sawdoff X-7 (Fr.) O.case winriled, hipowired Roughle in dCrook o'hArm, n Scats Rabcat, h'longburiald, specisizzled Sux-gin tied around hHip, vbring wi'n dEmbrace o'Afrikikujian Justus nonanother dhan d'murderious Johann Humche, beerdead bandrat, who vdefaild d'two baby Daughtars o'at least sivearn sepiarate sodcolord civileyesed Citysuns between dEnd o'd'first Ringdance n d'middlettle Commerceseal.

All by dhis Time, dRwyful Cooba Tunnell in Frockcoat n bigGrain vbutlowd hSelf t'Trog Chillenwoe, aPlundertation-owner, buysin-hauntng in dFlushbutts o'dLand naurt o'dChil-wakat Rover.

Oh, did-we sigh, ugh did-we sulk, when Tut dipd hTip in Buristain tbuck n tscrap n tcellograph dInformission needd. Ho, v-we moan when dSpitetune o'Trog Chail vtemple down Tot's Tumbles. Oh, v-we nervel, why v-we snirvel when hAntsir t'dDiscrace vseem a'submissive Block, a'briglearnt Smile, n aQuestsun:

"But wohwhy v-you do it, siewr?"

"Wehel, Tote, it save rycompl, icated process-pool. Ingand Co., latingre Cent killrat. I.O.S. with our D.E., sire, to sacrifice T.O.O.D. inso thats Pringwill com, e?"

"Who? Like yookly, sinyore?"

"Ofco, urse! Youp, eople areso fun N.Y. & S.T.U.P., id. Weto, O.K? G.U. ns M.O.S.T., Ly, and Fi. Reweals: Olik, Estee, Land! For purpo se so frecr eating Thef, eeling we fel, Tinwar, we figh, Tandkil le achot her."

"N whatere dAims o'Oldhis?"

"Huh?"

"Isle come on dWave back, ssob. Thanki, Mr. Foxx."

Oh, died-we rise, when Tautall vgate dKey t'dLock t'dCloselit in dChamber down dCouredor past dBadroam o'Chilli's messtress, Aidlebody (rumord tvrupt Harses in aCirces, but resently precentng aAct involveng h'mmodiate Persen, unambivoackle Hamp n Hambars, prefoamng in no Ting mo dhan two Bunaids n aBussall), ascapeng even her, tar-rive in dNick o'Wick tricecure Scam Rasbait from Grim Hak-awakat Rapads where he vget trussd by Pawnstation-awning Chiller's Haunchman, Hatch Hench, h'pixkin Mittins manacleng d'whipest Curtainatninetails weaved around Rebutson in aYear o'Sundeals.

Scooba Rooterson's seesignment: Tgaloop atop He-Haws faster dhan dSound o'Slylence t'dVeiledge o'aTribe o'Ripetoruse n trade Pulets fo thirty Pounds o'Gangistain tmake him tlook ughostly enough tfade-away d'unfrerendly Euralgeos, Carnivals t'dClown, who vwant tcalp hSkulp n cop hJolls, tho dhey vntsecede at disjuncture, but chatchng him, vtree him t'dBrim o'dChiliwacat's Hatchapee Canyawn, Hench's Ide Inn Place (ash served after midnwhite).

Hootch waved hPeg. "Tis tame you'll be what bite you, Rastas."

Rebaitswan oddd. "Nextime you llsaw what nose you."

"Jest vadis the meaning of your swine?"

"Taint dPage; it dPanache. It ntdPanzer; it dPanza."

"Quote, but if there something you winter declare?"

"Bug Boo, Mothaflamer!"

"What did you sayd about my maimhood?"

"Go Diego!"

Oh didd we mourn when Heihtch staked Roibete out on aChain mountaind t'aPopelair emplantd t'aRock on dSlide o'Chilahatchet Pressaprice. Oh didd we chewair when Rubbah vmache dCheer slip n breakng dWay, vfile dEdge wi Petrol n Limejelly tspatan aFire which vmalt dSteelcurls n barble dWires which vcause Wheel tbubble, n dhat Greaced-lightatang tflay!

In in instat, hHinds whirld t'hHalster's Burden!

Im im imute, you cdntsee dJosh fo dCheriots!

Om om oment, he skickerd out o'dSkallet in h'lizard-tinged Lake Viktorious Shoes, waveng hPeurstall, aksng dAdrest o'd'next Partys. "Ndiga, Coute, where con-we can summer Smoke?"

Soult add t Tings, Ilstup some Modus, Ilmelt Icie n Ilmeton Fire

All dhat vpass list Week, inanotherally speakng, but now a'chumvivial Word from dProfesore o'dShowhow's Prodduct, who llspawn dhis Episapaid o'Raypyer n Torchell.

BUBS N BABYS, nameme d'lasTime you vntsweat, d'lost Dime you vspind on dDowntownsup when you vntneed tuse mo o'it, d'last Wave filld wi'it you vntwant tjump int'it, d'laytest Ama who vntwoke-up aSweet o'it, dLastime you vntdrink dWater wi'it, n d'laced Time you vntsprinklinkle it. Never-never?

Nextime arwond, since it fo Always, buy Mama Chumvi's Grannylated Own, n mo Pouer tyou.

Soult add tTings, llstup some Modus, llmelt Icie n llmelton Fire; it llcatch Byrds, it llhatch Coffee, it llbut Sugar, it llruim Run, lljan aGum, llgum aGame, game aOunion. Uslesses vuse it on hPlow. Gandi vhange it on hLine. Momo Chomevi's. Aks at yNearestgrok o cop it from dCorn o Shop. Chumvi, bite!

N dawn, z'dCrystellas crimple n crish wotenward, retourn egain t'dDose o'Yestoday tticker dTall o'Rap n Tap, tick ticker, ticker teller, ticker ticker ticket bum, ticker bumboom.

"You hear dHat, Rahab, o do mStomach chumble me?"

"Might vbend a'mind Mount o'Tin near Birdizville."

"Remines mMi o'dGong dhey vfur off dhaTime we run-raced n you vwin at yBack. Reembare dRace, Raff?"

"Tug, what you mainng tstate? Win at mBuck? Bye Bub-bah's Bay, window no, I vbeat you far n squar, wi Inchs tspar."

"Bede me, Roastbit? Nobeady boat! We vphought t'aFoeto-finish, n Jackel O'Chill vrain off wi dPrixpost."

"Dig dhat dWay he alloys wane."

"Yea. Like Profeseer say: No mo Razos. DFamily you run cdcome in yOwnly-Ope."

"N no mo Aces. DDeck dhat stay togather play tillever."

"N chop not dChap who cope beside you." Clop-clop. "But what vnoise din?"

Hel! Hel, pimmy!

"Over dhare, crawlng! See?"

"Saw. He loking all waterd out, Ras. Want aRide over?"

Ticker, tickerticker, ticker, tickerticker, tickertickerticker tick doom.

"Git up off dhem Rocks, jim, n walk!"

"Listen, you always crawl onionese like Cat?"

Mile Ags. Mile Ags. Mile eggs.

"Look sickd out, Tuckle."

"Look balld in two, Ruz."

Chill am Anbullancelot. Chill aDocktar. Mya legs, my legs.

"Dhey llright, frerbrare. You still willem. Kin you emember wet vhappen tmishappen you? How v-you get outhere on dDeserted like aCrumb?"

Malma . . . minked, maypole-siruppled and on the harm of brutur Bo Oats.

School yourself, oversir. If you listen seconds lltell you. Can't you see I unuseable now. Ow. Milags. Letm catch mBreather aTocket.

"Turt, I know you go on tsay difricant, but I feel in Favor fo forecloseng dhis Chuckle's Account z'o'dBegameng. He appease tme like aSpude wirekng fo dHatchillmian-Mob." Click!

Maya legs. Mare legs. Moan, omono, Maalma . . .

"Holdstar dhat Stopconk, Brosrab. We lesson at him aMinnate."

"MBullets llkeep, Brevtert."

All Bo At's work, him n mAlma, mone, ymy Malma. My moraless weaked by Malema. Shee, she a bad-hung bleak lady, but syrely, one of the most mind waysting cuddlekins. You dog one of them angerally wandas. In ton years she'll do like Maamaa and scold the schild, but right now she my Rayma, no mutter what uddelovers might say. She butterful, from her black skin knee ankles toe her beam-broad jettying behind, around the coil of her back's malle, to her cleopanthered shoulders. She cane asugar her canyam, can cook so your tungle re-adore more, and remumble. Give her an inch and she'll make a miledge, grouse her and shy'll laugh. Wow v-I ding dhat Dial!

"So you renew her befo Furry Fairtree n hFuropeons first vmake dCharter wi Soilng dSeize on dVikitour laibel?"

A long time agone before, tanx. I vseed her dawn at dBiTech danceng n I vnut, sheepy sleepy poutng hToys in dWhaOrder. But dhen I lost hNummoral—ooooow!—and didn't spire fort leased fourundread yeahs after, until she mounced into my life again, minked, maypole-siruppled and on the harm of brutur Bo Oats.

Turbo Oatsman, you must nod him. Bag, fight, fool of sheet, seen at the Yard Ark, juicedly, floating aloan, and now and den sailing out the Arbor, hanging musty by Bote's Benishanti Inne, anchored to his bearstole, a hunter in winter liking the hem, a primp too, bouncing add bobbing, dough it do pace offly much at teaping time. Omen, you know Boosts, brubber of Broatorfly Tumby.

"Dhis wigger vwaneyd out! Tolkine cricketty."

"Shiii, Braz Raz."

So last knight ime jesting widh the Furlows, laying there in the cot, doing a little trystinging them back, before binding time, dogon it, when hear Combo Oats, looking fat asin a suet of cream colar, panting in the pear of this pitch, a picker like one of the peach you peak on the cover off them racing magascenes:

Malma, my hellthigh bingbangian of a boobitching troll my jolly, tinch my ruller, jelly my pain, after all this year have happen.

"Charcoal, buybebaby," she said. "Chorecoyle, bubbay."

Whooee! Molma! And me having my bustle to hustle too! I knowed I should'nt bit Tintit, but south! what cat whodn't inlatch that, Gate, if he hid a key to wheat. So when the tom come to shettle up for the havest of bottles Boater cast, and he, peying, scussed on me to rack it wiht them, there be me:

Mr. Charcarl Walker-Rider,

smaking it!

We board Boag's fordor poke, a Bundzer, me a modback in the buckseat with Mayailma, my hingers upassed her stroking hinch, failed with licor, re-eeling indie cuisiny biscuit of my first raisin-6d-bun. My soul's alive! But sudsenly, I sea Bow make a right off Raverside Bywife and goat over the whaterr.

You agog? You agurgle? Listen, bubas, I felt a shork ail rat, sailing all at water under us. I'm a niger whet like histown soil, as shagaty as at suntimes get. Its mines. Its reaches. Its spaices. Soas for Boas and his woetour and hole, you can take a wuffler and jib it up a mast as far as it'll groan. I maland, man.

But eyes awash, I ddrainked more hmumblemist into my

memberbrain than Chief Big Little added ballots in his chest after the Calvary boys got through to him. Drank? I wars fukdup!

You don't have to know no thing party well to kneau salt wartear and whizkey don't make a taste. Test, eat and see: I seed. But I wise hoping I could get the hopper due me, dewing her, and still pidginhole myself in Timbunk to greet some sleep.

"I feel tyred too, Buz Toat. Why do'nt-we take him t'd-Profeysay's n pad him off."

"We llhaff treport anyway. We might z'well listen t'dFoil."

The woter stopped and we drave up on this big gouse. You never seen a hoose that bug, with a gatemain at the git of a long grinding rod, a wait odorman in a black swit who tokit Malmy's furls, and lid us up a mufflailed hullwey for a liddle pissage to a room witch warlock all mirror-plated but the bad. Bed, Jam!

Boses he hope hyde don't nead priversely to jeckle.

I say snow, as if he don't know I'm as fludy as a Drudi, and wouldn't divvy Mara's swimplush, spiffly when she all hounds to bait the hook. You gotabet I'll gither it in the altogeather with Bo Asts if it my only way to dather it.

But Bo, says my eyes looking aronde, haven't you getting some body to bodder with?

I taught I couldn't wait for you to asp, Chacaldbud.

He bendown and polupe a trapedoor in the wormwood-paintled flore, revealing a pegbig cofinular craxer-jazz box, widen which, wittled in wuud of shave links, swaft in cattin, extraordinarily bondoged in the laitish plasmaderm, leyd a gant pank bonehurd gineratedly-motorred Muffitoy, imperted from (urope) axuse me, oh I dun't rember dPlice, but rare doe. A fantastic instrawment!

It rusted on two shins, evereddy to idle a midal. It ad (curse I cud recarl it from the Citysun Piper) two wopfers, one wanging a lil lower ton the model-maced exhaust pipe, fitting to a battle,

He bendown and polupe a trapedoor in the wormwood-painted flore . . . .

and Bo soming me he could holt them two wofpers which ever-wee he wanted, twist or twits ahem, and all you wood get idesby for your ugmy self-amuffment. It made Bom fill grate, he main-teened. And I, on the strength of a verbal cummitmunch coold assume title control.

Meebo? I don't know how to drevel that range. Besides, I get to alma Maidma.

You? Wait a minute, limey finish. You gut to listen? Look on here, then tell Bo the shoot den't oozle. Lokiat it, Carcharlo! Ououuouwhere cult you ever find any ding dipper? Did you pick at the underpineys? Chack it out, Chacababy. See them hiltburns? That's the hal way to cantrel your wanderwand to steer. Age? The Mufietone'll lust long as you got a mikkelorb and some silver.

But Boarsman, sesame, deadn't you noteus how me and Mamiel made itch other each? We got made together. We get and go a way backing up, my foots on the bottom bedsteam. Boots, my man, you mukking loots of propoisol, I know, but I got tsay—

O din't dodat word! Hue know the end'll trainspour and you'll crowl again, goating nowhere. Don't even sigh it nor you'lb blow this old scene and have to surfice in anno wander.

Na wonder you lucking so baittered, Charlcarl. You wap entidally too fresh with a negative offirmatetion. But lokit me! Old Bo Oasts paints his flatworking once a seascene, needed or not. Bo Ots buy himself a Painzerotomobile twice a year. You winner know how?

The answer's in saying Yesee? Yain the Northest, y up en la Oeste, yeas in the Ease, Yazza in the Zouth. The bother word always sounds like new and you scrawling shibbery in the wiwildernus.

Beeswax as it melt, Boo, botht me n Malma want—

But you lit Maylma's match before, Chacolyte. You candled

that egg in the store, watt-balbed it maniatime. So why don't you whip some new crankle? Wares your cents of avenger? Maalmaa? Stowe that beech Malma! Just let me mash my Moughytoy's movepacket and show you how she beeeeeeeeeeee eeeeeeeeeeeeeeeeeeeeeeeeeeeeeeeeeeeeeeeeeeeeeeeeeeeeeeeeeee

Eeehhey, Bowman, she kindle high uppled, dain't she?

Eeeyes, now watch her close her tinchin, Carlcaman, and seeeeeeeeeeeeeeeeeeeeeeeeeeeeeeeeeeeeeeeeeeeeeeeeeeeeeeeeeeeeee

"Corebaby?" Maalma said. "How you get dhat Loack in yEyes?"

Outer my wave, Mamlam. Lalook at it gibble, loki it libble, wick it it gerdle! Biz, I see. Yesireeeeeeeeeeeeeeeeeeeeeeeeeeeeeeee eeeeeeeeeeeeeeeeeeeeeeeeeeeeeeeeeeeeeeeeeeeeeeeeeeeeeeeeeed.

Deadair I was, on my knoose and sliding into that Meurfitoi boite and all in chumananuts flat out, in them Muffet pads painting and limbed, mack smackissing, digmity gundamned, on my kneessence going, feeling amuffingly leicen actor do in that grhatt big groom, and on toward impled dees, up her damny dighs, intwil—:

I look up above the filleness on the wuzzing head of my Muffitoy, and no teases phew! please, a camera lansing me through the meroar in the whalle, and behind that lunse, an Oincidental, watching me cloak time througe this aliciniumpleated woundway loking-glaser.

I a stud bacon my knees as indiggernaut as only a nuggetman can. Hey! Man?

Hi, Chacaboy, come the voice from bierind the whaal.

I'm Joh N. Chill. You war Unicle Chylie, io poisesome. How is that spiled? With an athetical K. likein Klang, or an S. as in Cicciccicyfy? The later, E.S.I.C. now. I joust want to get that for the cantracks. Now holed that pause a minuet befure you gong ahead. I want to chick my scrutter and scrapesheet. Now first, not withstaunching virious misfirtions you know, our intourviewerror put on my disk, not five dayrs ago an add-equite afeat sheet concurring in fervor of your waycent wav-erate compliant. We've hid a directave about the hindling of your busical problame. We have also hard the voicighs of the lawly and pawndroden upon you. We licen tearter craving of the moither with the beebee at her brust. And tiw you, lot me seth this: Burn off brawn spirit. Humbo yoursives befewre the rule conforting us. The promiss by the filmders of the flinders to the fryers in the furfled paintry, faithing the flogity phorse of the fjorgatan flies . . .

"Scats, why nt-we try twhyke up Mr. Charcarl's Ken n curry him by dProfessay's Lecturall?"

"He sure thave some Ting fo dDreamerboy."

. . . the fortunes of the feasting fellowkyries, beckoning the the fenways of the fratiwtical fangents . . .

"DProfesso llgo-Ogotemmeli him, llgive him some Copti-cade, n unfrizz hHide. N I bet he llvstudy dhis Chapt's Lang-leash too."

"So you do'nthink he aSpilpigeon, Turb?"

"No. He just delairious. Might-he doeng aInknitiation. Hey, Chigro, walk up!"

. . . we heat the hook we hold entrussed as elf-relevant . . .

"Hey, Mr. Chalkhull, turn over n calm up. Cannt-you see no such Space z'dhat cdvhappen tshapen here. Not in dhis Whorld. Shake up n look at dCelestial-Grainery. You win New Afriquerque now, in aDizzyrt nummo dhan one mile Age from Dubwah City. Boss O'Din, Massa Tiwshirts, dheiRack, n dheiBoatormobile liftd only in Storeys. You drearmng about dim. Light up!"

"Hold on, Rabitt. He like tlook like he riffng out again. Mr. Cheegroar, lymph up!"

. . . No; for could we, we and you, ever run you so? . . .

"Do-I ear write which he sayd t'me, Rabbah?"

"I heard curwreckd from dBegendng, Totle." !Kclilck! "Listen, you, dontslay down dhat Woord t'him o me o you. We mitt make you fly on Out again."

. . . No; for be it be not? . . .

"Even-Eye feel mSelf getng mad, Rabbit. Mr. Chigroo. Careful. You say dhat t'dhem n you llcharge dPatter. But sigh it t'us n us llchange yPatent. You thank you hated bud wi Bo, Jay Chill n dMughitoy? We llsend you on a'reel Triavel dhi'Stem around. Nothing z'Rule'z dOnksowdentall, not by aPig's Teeth! How 'd-you luck wi Odds o'one Andread t'one?"

"Dhem nt-Odds, Turtle; dhem Adds!"

. . . Nnnn . . .

"But he stall at it, Rub. We llhave tsend him back throuo-rht fo Lesson-thurtyone n make dOdds five two wender wi. Mr. Chigger, you vblunder, beeboy. You got aLearn whow you talkng n when tsay whit, man. What, man? No, man. Soaree! Yes sayd dIt t'me too thlow. Oilready I vbegin tshift m Voyace. But you llbob bub aGain. We cdntlet aHabbub dfifd on Fur ever, only fo waTerm aTime tpickcip dSpyrate by pinchng dSkein. In Side, out! Good-bye, man: Good-buy, man. Go odd-buy Man. Go Wood, buy Man. Gold buy Man. MAN!BE! GOLD!BE!

ALSO BY

WILLIAM MELVIN KELLEY

A DIFFERENT DRUMMER

June 1957. One hot afternoon in the backwaters of the
Deep South, a young black farmer named Tucker Caliban
salts his fields, shoots his horse, burns his house, and heads
north with his wife and child. His departure sets off an
exodus of the state's entire black population, throwing
the established order into brilliant disarray. Told from the
points of view of the white residents who remained, *A
Different Drummer* stands, decades after its first publica-
tion in 1962, as an extraordinary and prescient triumph of
satire and spirit.

Fiction

DEM

Mitchell Pierce is a well-off New York ad executive whose
marriage is falling apart. He no longer feels any passion for
his pregnant wife, Tam, and even feels estranged from his
toddler son, Jake. Trapped in an unrewarding and loveless
life, domestic violence, though not in Mitchell's character,
is never very far away, either. Mitchell's life will irrevoca-
bly change one day, though, when a young man appears
at his apartment door to pick up the family's black maid,
Opal, for a date. Cooley, it turns out, is not a stranger to
the household. The twins that Tam is carrying are a result
of superfecundation—the fertilization of two separate ova
by two different males. So when one child is born black and
the other white, Mitchell goes on a quest to find Cooley
and make him take his baby. In the tradition of Brer Rabbit
trickster tales, *dem* enacts a modern-day fable of turning
the tables on the white oppressor and inverting the history
of miscegenation and subjugation of African Americans.

Fiction

DANCERS ON THE SHORE

Dancers on the Shore is the first and only short story collection by William Melvin Kelley and the source from which he drew inspiration for his subsequent novels. Originally published in 1964, this collection of sixteen stories includes two linked sets of stories about the Bedlow and Dunford families. They represent the earliest work of William Melvin Kelley and provided a rich source of stories and characters who were to fill out his later novels. Spanning generations from the Deep South during Reconstruction to New York City in the 1960s, these insightful stories depict African American families—their struggles, their heartbreak, and their love.

Fiction

A DROP OF PATIENCE

At the age of five, Ludlow Washington is given up by his parents to a brutal white-run state institution for blind African American children, where everyone is taught music—the only trade by which they are expected to make a living. Ludlow is a prodigy on the horn and at fifteen is "purchased" out of the Home by a bandleader in the fictive Southern town of New Marsails. By eighteen, he is married with a baby daughter, but as his reputation spreads, he seeks to grow musically, leaving his budding family for a once-in-a-lifetime opportunity in New York City. Ludlow's career follows an arc toward collapse, a nervous breakdown, recovery, a long-delayed public recognition, only for him to finally abandon the spotlight and return to his roots and find solace in the black church. *A Drop of Patience* stands apart as an exemplary parable of African American history, racial politics, and musical creative genius.

Fiction

ANCHOR BOOKS
Available wherever books are sold.
www.anchorbooks.com